# FURNACE

For Archie,
with all my best,
Wayne.

# FURNACE

*Wayne Price*

**FREIGHT
BOOKS**

First published in the UK Feb 2012
By Freight Books
49-53 Virginia Street
Glasgow, G1 1TS
**www.freightbooks.co.uk**

A CIP catalogue reference for this book is available from the British Library
ISBN 978-0-9566135-8-5

Typeset by Freight in Plantin
Printed by Martins Printers, Berwick

the publisher acknowledges investment from
**Creative Scotland** toward the publication of this book

*For Ali*

# THE GOLFERS

When my older brother Alfie left school for good he got a job collecting up the balls out at the airbase golf range. He couldn't learn how to drive the little electric cart they normally used but he helped out on foot, lugging a great sack behind him like a baby-faced Santa, ducking too late when anyone sent a ball close and bothered to yell. I think they took him on as a favour to my mother's boyfriend from those times, a pink-skinned, sandy-haired sporting type whose name I can't recall now. Anyway, this boyfriend drank and golfed with some of the airmen who practiced there. Or maybe it was my older sister Carol who fixed it for him. She drank with plenty of airmen too.

In late July of that year sudden, incredible rains flooded the river and all the brooks around town and then, just as suddenly, a freakish, continental heat set in. The air felt baked and stifling, not just in the day but for hours into the dark. At thirteen, the feel of that weather was entirely strange to me, and ominous. I've never forgotten it. In all the back yards giving on to water a kind of eggshell glaze, pale orange from iron oxide in the local streams, topped the fine silt left behind from the floods. There was a wide expanse of it left at the foot of the empty schoolyard, a place I often escaped to in the summer holidays. I spent one wholly absorbed morning there, treading out long careful lines of footprints in the weirdly perfect, pastel casing that covered the black asphalt and sports markings. It was like breaking the crust of some virgin, alien world.

Like any sudden change, the strangeness of the weather was bad for Alfie. Early one morning I wandered into the kitchen and found him transfixed at the window, sweating in the sun. He was waiting for Carol to take him out to the golf range on her way to work. Only his right arm was moving, like part of some machine – jerking up and down between his throat and hip, a spasm every few seconds. Each time the hand went up, the big pink fingers went fluttering over the tight collar button of his shirt. His round face was sheened over and puffy and he grunted quietly each time he touched the fastening. His eyes were bulging, almost glassy, but he never went open-collared, not even at home. Not even in pyjamas. I watched him for a minute or so.

Oh just open it for Christ's sake, I said at last.

But then Carol yelled through from the hall – Alfie, I'm going! Get in the car! And he went, lunking past me same as he always did like I hadn't said a word.

\* \* \*

Later that same day Jez and Fisher call round. I'm hiding from the sun, living room curtains drawn tight, sweating into the sofa and sipping from one of my mother's bottles of sweet blue liquor. Both Jez and Fisher are Alfie's age, three years older than me, and only sometimes want me around. When the doorbell rings – one heavy, drawn-out chime – I know it's Jez. My head's swimming a little from the drink, making it hard to stand up quickly. The bell goes again, even slower this time – someone's finger grinding on the face of the button. Once, a single fat turd came through our letterbox on Halloween, and whenever Jez rings the doorbell the way he does I remember seeing it there on the doormat and feel like I know for sure it was him.

Jez takes the bottle out of my hand as he moves past me into the hall. What's this? he says, and fills his mouth with it.

It's spirits, I tell him, watching his face.

His lips pull back tight over his teeth.

It's my mother's, I say. But it's strong. Check out the label.

He ignores me and passes the bottle to Fisher. Taste that, he says.

He moves restlessly around the living room, picking things up and putting them back somewhere different. Then Fisher settles himself on the edge of the sofa, tilts himself forward and takes a couple of really big neckfuls, sucking at the bottle like a baby on a tit. When he swallows I can see the gulps moving under the fat.

Let's go, I say.

They glance at one another and laugh.

The heat outdoors is a shock even though I'd been sweltering inside. The tarmac's cooking along the sides of the gutters and the thick oily smell of it seems to carry up off the road with the heat shimmers, rolling along with us as we walk.

It's not long before we leave the streets and wander into the back-alleys near the allotments and the old railway line. The flies are worse there, but at least the tar-pit stink is gone. Jez and Fisher are hanging back from me, like they usually do, plotting and sniggering. It doesn't bother me much, though sometimes I slow up to eavesdrop and check if they're planning anything bad for me. Now though, Jez catches up with me and whips the backs of my legs with a thin branch he picked up somewhere.

Hey Nicky, he says, where's Carol hanging out these days?

I shrug.

She still working out on the estate?

Yeah.

A fat summer bluebottle razzes right across our faces. I flinch back but Jez doesn't even seem to notice.

What time does she finish?

I take a quick look at Jez, sideways on. How would I know? I say, trying to sound calmer than I feel. I pull some air back in and try to whistle.

He grins, showing his teeth. They're tiny and very straight. Just tell me what time she gets home, he says.

Most days she picks up Alfie and then brings him home with her, so they get in about six.

Jez suddenly stops walking. Big Alfie's got a job? he says, amazed. Hey Fish – Alfie's got a job!

Fisher gives out a loud, false laugh from a little way behind us. A job! *Alfie!* he crows.

Jez starts walking again, but he's interested now and leaves off swiping at me. So where's he working? he asks.

I tell him about the job at the golf range and he just walks quietly alongside me for a minute or so, thinking about something. It's funny, eh? he says. You and Alfie.

I don't say anything because I know exactly what's coming.

I mean Alfie being just a big soft fucking retard. And then you. He looks me up and down as we walk. The sly professor, eh? He swishes the branch onto the backs of my legs again. Little Professor Pinkdick.

Yeah right, I say.

Then there's Carol, eh? And when I don't answer again he turns his head and calls back to Fisher – hey Fish, what about Carol, eh? What about Carolingus?

Yee-hah! Fisher shouts, and when I turn back to look at him he spits straight up in the air and scoots under it, grinning all over his white fat face. He carries on jogging so that he catches up with us.

It's having different fathers, Jez pronounces.

Yeah right, I say again, sweating even worse now.

That's why though, he says, seriously. It fucks up all the natural stuff. It's why you're hot for your own fucking sister. That's right, Fish, right?

Fisher sniggers.

That's what it is, professor, believe me.

We carry on in silence for a time. Jez maybe senses he's gone too far because he starts switching the branch at Fisher's legs instead of mine.

Nicky, you ever been out to the golf range? he says at last.

No, I lie.

They've got pitch and putt out there, behind the range.

I shrug.

Jez slows up with Fisher and soon they've dropped back behind me again, conferring, and I'm on my own trying to stop the flies landing on my head and neck in case they follow the trails of sweat and end up inside my T-shirt.

Around noon we've drifted right along to where the railway used to cross the river. Without saying anything we scramble down the embankment, through dusty gorse and broom and bramble bushes, until we're in amongst the big river rocks left high and dry by the low water. We stop there for a smoke, sitting on the warm boulders. What's left of the river curls away green and quiet between the broken pillars of the old viaduct. It feels peaceful to be there, sitting and smoking in the sun. Even Jez looks relaxed, watching the smooth run of the river, letting the smoke come lazy out of his mouth and nose.

Then, somehow not making a sound, Fisher vomits onto the rock between his legs. He keeps his head down a minute while Jez stares. A cord of sticky blue stuff links his chin and lips with the mess on the boulder but it's like he doesn't have the energy to spit it clear.

Christ's sakes, Jez says, turning back to the river again. Let's go play golf.

It's a long walk in the heat but Jez makes us tramp all along the road to Milo's garage at the edge of town before he lets us get on one of the small airbase buses. We're the only locals on board – the well-dressed airmen's wives with bulging carrier bags and the airmen in civvies are all on their way back to their quarters on the base. Jez spreads himself wide to take up the whole of his double seat and smokes, though the whole bus is no-smoking. After a while one of the women starts giving him disgusted looks, but the airmen in front of us don't seem to care and nothing gets said.

Fisher keeps pretty still all through the ride, looking down at his feet like he's concentrating hard. I wonder if he'll throw up my mother's booze again, but he keeps it in.

The big wooden sign advertising the range is just a few hundred yards in front of the sentry boxes guarding the base. I notice it before Jez or Fisher and stand up to ask the driver to stop. He eyes me without saying anything, but slows down anyway and lets us off. As I step down to the grass verge one of the airmen sitting near the driver says something I don't catch, and the driver lets out a quick sharp laugh.

Behind the sign a rough gravel track runs straight and very flat between two fields to a line of low sheds in the distance. That must be it, Fisher says, almost the first words he's spoken since the river.

It is, says Jez.

Far off in the base a jet engine starts to whine, builds to a kind of howl as we start walking, then dies down again without anything getting airborne.

Soon we start passing faded wooden boards marking out yardages. White golf balls, some of them split and showing their pink insides, are nested everywhere in the dried-out patchy grass. A car passes us, crunching over the grit and pebbles, carrying three airmen in uniform.

Another follows a few seconds later, this time with just a single woman driving. Both cars get to the sheds, then swing left and park. By the time we reach the end of the track the airmen and the woman have unloaded their gear and disappeared through the nearest doorway. We follow them into the shade.

Ahead of us the woman is crouched at some kind of battered steel vending machine. She pulls sharply at a handle and a quick landslide of golfballs rumbles and fills a wire basket at her feet. She heaves the basket up in one hand, three or four golf clubs in the other, and hauls it out to a line of wooden bays like wide open toilet stalls. Fisher squats down and snakes a hand up the funnel where the balls fell but doesn't get hold of anything. Jez and me look across at the woman and the airmen in their stalls. The woman's stretching herself, bending sideways from the waist, grimacing, but the men have stripped off their uniform shirts and are already cracking long, arcing shots into the blue sky.

A guy calls to us from a doorway near the machine: You boys needing clubs? Balls?

We need everything, Jez tells him.

The guy nods. He looks about fifty – fat but tough-looking with a big shaved head. An oily black and grey beard is spread in a mess all over his cheeks and chin and neck. It's two pounds per club, he says, his eyes fixed on Jez. Fifty pence if you lose a ball. He scratches the right side of his beard, from the cheekbone all the way to his collar, waiting for one of us to say something. When we don't, he reaches into a pocket on the faded blue boiler suit he's wearing and fishes out a pack of smokes. He's already turned to go back through the doorway when Jez tells him we'll hire a club to share between us.

He stops and turns back to face us. Pitch and putt or the range?

Jez shrugs. Which is cheapest?

Pitch and putt. He rolls his tongue around the inside of his mouth, then draws on his cigarette. You got balls?

I'm expecting Jez to give him a smart answer but he just shakes his head. A ball too, he says.

One ball? You don't want a ball each?

Just one, says Jez.

The man sighs out a big stream of smoke and then leads us into his office. A row of cheap-looking golf clubs are lined up behind his battered wooden counter. Newer bundles of clubs, gleaming and with price tags on them are set against a side wall along with some golf bags, a half-filled barrel of balls and a couple of shelves of spiked shoes. The room smells of leather for some reason, maybe because of the shoes. You'll want this for the pitching, he says, handing Fisher a club from the row behind the counter. And you'll need this for the putting. He hands another, smaller club to me. He turns to Jez. You can have a damaged range ball for free or you can use a new one and pay up if it gets lost. What'll it be? He takes a deep drag, then taps delicately into a small, overflowing ashtray.

What's the difference?

He grunts. You won't tell the difference.

A new ball.

The big guy pushes his tongue around his mouth again. Right son, he says.

Jez takes the clubs and then waits while Fisher and me dig enough money out of our pockets to pay for them. All the time the guy watches us, especially Jez. When we're done he points us out of the shop towards a fire-escape door propped open with a half-brick. Through there, he says.

To start with we get the whole course to ourselves. From the first tee-mat, perched up on a dusty mound, we can see every one of the nine holes and they're all deserted except for a big, lumbering figure hauling a rake over one of the miniature bunkers six or seven holes away.

Alfie, announces Jez.

Call him over, says Fisher, smirking.

Jez shakes his head. We'll catch up with him, he says, and drops the bright new golf ball onto the rubber mat at his feet. He's not going anywhere, he adds. And sure enough, for all the time we watch him, Alfie's rake drags over and over the same little patch of sand like a stuck needle on a record.

Out of the corner of my eye I can see the guy with the beard watching from the shed doorway. Hit the ball, Jez, I say.

Jez spreads his arms wide, keeping us out of his sight line, then steadies himself, feet wide apart and knees locked. He takes a wild heave and misses, pounding the rubber mat so hard a big, chalky puff of dust comes up. Fuck off, that was practice, he mutters when Fisher makes a move for the club. He sets himself rigid again then beats down even harder, this time getting the ball to spurt off twenty yards or so along the yellow grass. He tells Fisher to fetch it back for him and I can feel the manager's eyes still boring into our backs.

By the time we get to Alfie, the airmen have finished with the range and are playing right behind us, hitting proper, high golf shots that thump down and bounce head-high off the hard ground as soon as we leave a green.

Alfie's excited to see me. Nicky! he barks out. I'm too hot and uptight to go to him but Jez and Fisher start slapping him hard on the back. Then they reach up to scrub their knuckles on the top of his head. Alfie's hunched up already, throwing me cowed looks that make my guts churn.

Suddenly, a golf ball whacks in amongst us and Jez and Fisher leave Alfie alone to jump away from the green. Hey! What the fuck? Jez yells back at the airmen. They shake their heads and one of them sends another ball thudding in front of us. We move off to a hole they've already played, Jez dragging Alfie along with us.

Fish, what's the time? he asks, and like I'm just waking up, I realise why we're here. Carol.

I move off a little way and sit down heavily on the rim of a bunker. I try to calm myself by just concentrating on my dusty shoes and the dirty rough sand round about them. This could be the desert, I think to myself. It could be Africa, or somewhere out of the Bible. I close my eyes and blood-coloured lights throb in and out of the black. I can hear Jez and Fisher getting Alfie to put down his rake and take hold of the golf club. He doesn't want to, but that just makes Jez more determined. I'm thinking I wish I could bury myself in the sand right here without anyone noticing, or disappear into a desert forever where no one knows anything about Alfie or Carol or me.

The thing that finally makes me look up is the guy from the shop coming over to check what's going on. Even then I only open my eyes because Fisher sends him over to me. It's okay, I hear him say, we're all just having fun. We're Alfie's friends. That's even his brother. That's his little brother over there.

The big guy walks over to me. I can hear his footsteps coming and that's when I look. You're Alfie's brother? he says.

I nod and look up but I can hardly see his face for the blood-lamps still drifting across my eyes.

He shakes his big untidy face. Leave him alone, he growls to all of us. He's got work to do. I catch you messing with him again, I'll mess with you, brother or no brother. Everyone understand?

He goes on staring at me for quite a while, but doesn't say anything else. In the end he turns and trudges back to the sheds.

I look over at the others. Alfie's got his rake back and he's stood in a bunker but looks like he's forgotten what to do. He keeps shrugging and repeating something quiet to himself, over and over, too quiet for me to hear the words.

Jez goes and rolls the ball onto the nearest tee-mat with his foot. You do it, he tells Fisher, and hands him the club. A jet screams low, leaving the base and climbing.

A Buccaneer, says Fisher, and his mouth stays open. They're just trainers, he goes on to no one in particular, disappointed, but he watches after it anyway until it's just a speck in the hot blue.

Hit the ball for Christ's sake, Jez tells him.

But neither of them care much now and Jez doesn't even crow when Fisher scuffs the ball sideways into long, dead grass. Fisher grunts, but not like it matters.

Then someone sets a car horn going, three long blasts, and I know it's Carol. Alfie knows it too – he shuffles out of the sand and makes for the sheds, leaving the rake half-cocked over the bunker's edge.

Jez and Fisher give each other a look then set off after him.

Where are you going? I call, my heart speeding.

Fisher mumbles something to Jez and laughs, then he turns and tosses the club to me. It lands upright with a bump, bounces and cartwheels into the bunker, just missing my legs. Jez keeps hold of the putter, swinging it from the metal head like a walking stick.

I stay where I am, churning my feet into the gritty sand. It seems to take forever before they all come trooping over to me – Carol first, then Jez and Fisher, then poor old Alfie following last with his big wide simple face, though now it's twitching with nerves.

Carol stops a couple of paces away from the bunker and sweeps her long fringe from the side of her face, holding it back for a second; then she lets it drop back exactly the way it was. Look after Alfie for a while, she says.

What?

You heard. Look after Alfie.

Why? I realise my feet are twisting more quickly now, but not getting any deeper, almost like they're waving at her out of their burrows. I stop it and pull them up clear. She looks at them hard, like they mean something.

Why? I say again.

I glare up at Fisher and Jez, both standing just behind Carol, one on either side. Fisher keeps darting quick looks from me to Carol to Jez and back again. Jez won't look me in the eye. He's looking kind of dreamily out over the airbase, though I know there's nothing to see.

We're just going for a drive, Carol says. With the windows down. To get cool. She flicks her hair back again. Ten minutes, she says.

I snort and she rolls her eyes.

Jez frowns in whatever kind of dream he's in, but still doesn't look at me.

Just mind Alfie, okay? Ten minutes, she says.

Fisher turns to wave and wink at me as they go.

Leave him alone, Carol says, sounding tired, and I watch their backs until they disappear round the side of the sheds, the long tin roofs shimmering in the heat.

I wait until the engine coughs and starts, then stand up and turn to Alfie. You're wondering where Carol's gone, I tell him.

He's staring after them, red-faced, big wet lips working slowly but not making words.

I get out of the bunker and stand on its brim. Over in the airbase compound a blue minibus is filling up with private-school kids in their dark grey air-corps uniforms. A tall, young-looking teacher in the same outfit slams the back doors behind them, jogs around to the driver's seat and climbs in. Then the bus just sits there on the hot black tarmac, not moving. Further out, on one of the distant runways, another Buccaneer accelerates, then roars into the air. It makes a low circle and thunders over the driving range before heading out towards the sea.

* * *

All these years on, and Alfie a long time dead, it's strange to think of the airbase, the jets and runways, hangars and fences all buried or broken up. All of it carried away like the whole thing was made of playing cards. It's grazing land now, rough and wide open and empty except for young heifers or sometimes a solitary, wandering bull. The driving range too of course: all vanished. Strange to think of thistles growing up tall and hooves cutting in where the combed white bunkers, neat fairways and smooth, clipped greens were. You take the quiet drive out there now to the headland and there's no way of knowing.

The ten minutes passed somehow. A couple of times I tried to distract Alfie from staring spellbound after them, but it didn't really help – whatever I said he kept his blank, wide-awake eyes fixed on the gravel road beyond the sheds. I picked the golf club out of the sand, found the ball in the tangled grass and chipped it up and down the little fairway a few times, back and forth. It was pleasant seeing the new white ball hop and roll so true on the neat strip of turf, shaved out so carefully from the scrub and thick weeds pressing in. It was the feeling of finding somewhere tended, cared for, where it didn't really need to be. It just was. Though we were in a place half the town and airbase had trampled over one Saturday afternoon or another, it suddenly felt set apart and private to us, and safe.

Is it you that cuts this grass? I called up the fairway to Alfie.

He rocked on his heels, still staring after Carol.

It's nice, I called again. Really nice.

I clipped the ball up the gentle slope towards him, then laid down the club and looked all around, standing tip-toe on the bunker's raised lip. The minibus with its uniformed kids was gone. We must have been waiting half an hour at least by that time. Alfie was grunting to himself, swaying almost imperceptibly from side to side. There was no sign of the car returning.

I'm not waiting, I said to Alfie, I'm going now, and to my amazement he followed when I started walking. I stopped and turned. Keep close to me and do what I do, I said, and for the first time in my life, as far as I remember, felt myself a companion to him. Soon, we'd climbed the golf course's white picket fence and were in open country. Behind me I heard the big, bearded manager call out after us but he didn't call for long and by the time Carol and Jez and Fisher must have spilled from her car we were out of sight and out of sound, swallowed up completely by the same spreading fields that come back always and would swallow up everything soon enough.

# THE WEDDING FLOWERS

It was a slow, hard climb through the Muslim graveyard. There was no path between the graves and the way was steep and shadeless, but it was a shortcut to the ruined chapel, saving at least half a mile, the English boy reckoned. Besides, he was desperate to escape the main route, winding and dusty, that followed the stream to the springs at Ras el Ma. All along the river, under the old town walls, gangs of brown, half-naked children had crowded the shallow pools, splashing and shrieking and begging when they noticed him; and above them, lining each pocket of shade above the path, lounged the older youths, interrupting their endless conversations to call out tirelessly as he passed, *'Hey, mon ami! Amigo! Hashish? Hey! My friend – good hash! Very cheap. Si? Hey, venez ici! Sit here. Yes? Hey!'* And always one or two standing and following until he reached the next strip of shade and the next gathering, the reek of *kif* heavy in the hot air again, and in every brittle tree and bush the invisible cicadas screaming as if on fire, and then a new volley of offers, and another stranger stalking behind him, dropping away only when the path twisted out of the shadows and into the painful glare of the sun, leaving him to the next link of shade and waiting smokers in the long, watchful, murmuring human chain. It was exhausting and he had chosen the shorter, steeper climb as soon as he'd noticed it, though it took him away from the river where he'd been able to drench his burning face and neck. His bottled water was already running low, but he could pace his drinking more carefully now that he was alone at last. He'd had to drink wastefully as he walked the gauntlet of the local youths, sucking from the bottle when they called out so that he'd seem preoccupied and purposeful. It was the same in the souks and markets of the medinas. In Tangier, Marrakech, Fez, and now here: always the bottle ready to seal his mouth, though he knew it was probably exactly that which singled him out as a tourist and brought him the attention he was warding himself against.

He stopped, wiped the sweat out of his eyes with the linen sleeve of his shirt and for the first time noticed properly the scattered, whitewashed graves surrounding him. They were almost identical: just narrow troughs of stone, around four feet in length. Even the largest were shorter and narrower than any adult coffin. The newest were dazzling under the late morning sun. At their ends they were stepped or arched, sculpted very simply and set low to the ground, many of them nearly hidden by the clumps of parched, wiry mountain grass that lay matted in between. A few carried short Arabic inscriptions but most were plain and there were no flowers, nor any other kind of offering, just pale gravel or more of the tough hillside grass inside the shallow walls of each rectangle. He wondered idly how deep the graves could be dug in the rocky soil. It looked unpromising: knuckles of grey Rif limestone jutted through the grass in every part of the burying ground. The clean, wordless graves were pleasing, though. Blank headstone after blank headstone, blocky and white, as if the blazing sun had bleached even their meanings away.

But Christ, it was hot. Too hot to linger in the open. The high sun seemed focused to a single, burning cone on the crown of his head and the glare and repetition of the white graves was making him dizzy. Just a few hundred yards further on, at the highest boundary of the graveyard, a skirt of trees fringed the last steep rise before the chapel. He could make for their shade or turn back and face the hustlers again at the river. With his left hand shielding the top of his head, he squinted up at the ruin and started to climb again.

The hunched figure sharing the shade of the trees, a little way above him and to his right, was silent, though the boy knew he was being watched as he dried the streams of sweat on his face, took a little water and recovered his breath. Behind them both, from the ruin, drifted the sound of cheerful Spanish voices. Eventually, two young couples carrying small, bulging day-packs on their backs came picking their way down a stony path between the shrubs and olive trees. The figure in the shade called out to them familiarly in Spanish and the two boys answered with laughs and a few fragments of conversation. It seemed to be the continuation of an earlier exchange, the English boy thought, though he could understand none of it except the *adios* the figure finally called out as they vanished into the scrub. Other than the endless background sawing of the crickets and cicadas there was silence for a while, then the sound of a match being struck. As if on cue, the stranger called over to him: *Amigo. Español?*

He turned and shook his head, examining the other man for the first time. No, he called back. The stranger was small and wiry, clearly a local. Older than the youths at the river, the boy decided - his scant goatee beard had streaks of grey in it, though the rest of his face was youthfully smooth and sharp-boned. He was staring again now, knees drawn up almost to his T-shirted chest, and smoking a black wooden sebsi. The smell of the struck match rolled by the boy, then the aroma of *kif*.

English? Yes?

The boy nodded.

The stranger grunted and puffed on the short pipe.

The boy turned away, ignoring the rattle of pebbles behind him as the Moroccan rose to his feet and made his way to the boy's side, settling himself on a smooth stone close by.

From London?

No. A smaller place. Nottingham.

Ah! Nottingham Forest. Brian Clough!

Despite himself the boy laughed. You've heard of him?

The stranger grinned toothily. All great coaches famous in Maroc!

The boy shook his head, still smiling. Dead now, he said.

Yes. You have smoke?

No thanks. I'm fine. He toyed with the cap of the bottle but resisted the impulse to open it and drink. The water was warm through the plastic and his fingers were slippery with sweat.

No smoke?

No. No smoke. I'm here to see the mountains.

Good. Very good. Many fine mountains here in the Rif. He cleared his throat. My name – Ibrahim, he announced abruptly, and reached over to offer his right hand.

The boy hesitated, then shook it. It was slender but the grip was strong. Hello, he said flatly.

For smoking I ask just once, said Ibrahim. In town, they say hash, hash, hash, yes? Always the hash. Me, I ask once.

Okay, the boy said. All around them the cicadas were deafening: an endless, grating chirr. It set the boy's nerves on edge the way a baby crying always did when he was a child.

Very hot, yes? Ibrahim went on. Rest before more walking.

Very hot, the boy agreed. Too hot.

Yes. Even for August. Very hot.

They fell silent for a while. A calm, watchful immobility seemed to settle on the stranger's face whenever he stopped speaking. It gave him a detached, superior air.

You live in town? the boy asked at last, uncomfortable with the silence. Without speech as a distraction, the cicadas' uproar was maddening.

In Chouen, no. My village – that way. Ibrahim pointed with the stem of his sebsi towards the broad stony valley running east from the town and the chapel. Sometimes I stay in Chouen, he added, and shrugged. You travel far in Maroc?

The boy nodded. I was in Tangier to start, then Fez and Marrakech, then headed back north. I was hoping it would be cooler in the mountains.

Ibrahim listened with a tilted head, as if straining to catch the words. He paused for a moment after the boy had finished speaking, then straightened his neck and grunted. Marrakech – too hot, he said. In Marrakech now, fifty-five degrees, maybe more. Centigrade, he added. Very bad. Better here. But today, not so good. Very hot in Chouen, too. He took several quick puffs on his pipe. Then, as if suddenly struck by the idea: I show you the mountains, yes? Show you the spring – cold water. Very clean. Good to drink. I know all the ways in the mountains. Good places for photographs. Very high up.

A wave of weariness and irritation ran through the boy but he fought to keep it from his voice. I don't know. I was planning on that anyway, you know? Walking in the mountains. You understand? I was going there anyway.

Of course, of course, said Ibrahim, smiling.

Well, okay, the boy finished lamely.

Of course. Ibrahim tapped the debris from his pipe. You see my village too, yes? I show you the farms where they make the *kif* and the hash. Tourists not permitted, but I take you.

The boy yawned helplessly. It was suffocatingly hot, even out of the sun, and being hustled always made him feel strangely drained. Ever since arriving in the country and breaking with his girlfriend who had taken an early flight home, he had become more and more aware of a weakness in himself, like a painless but sapping wound that each hustle opened up afresh; now, sensing it opening again he felt a wave of despair. He closed his eyes, remembering his first night in Tangier. Within minutes of strolling onto the palm-lined Corniche he'd been cajoled by two guides into buying his evening meal at an empty beach restaurant where they'd promised he could find cold beer. They'd plied him with fresh sardines, American beer and pipes of *kif* until well past midnight, then pretended to collect the bill from inside the bar before presenting him with a crudely scribbled note in Arabic demanding more money than he'd set aside for a week's accommodation. When he'd tried to reason with them they'd called the big, taciturn waiter to the table and the boy had understood, suddenly fearful, that all three of them were in on the scam. The most bewildering part of it though was that once he had paid, defeated and furious, the two guides had acted as if nothing untoward had happened. They'd insisted on escorting him back to his hotel, making friendly, broken conversation and the younger one had been completely at ease jostling at his shoulder, even showing off the creased scraps of paper, scrawled with names and addresses of various foreign girls, that he kept stuffed in a bulging nylon wallet. As they'd approached his hotel a café-owner, watching the late night stragglers along the Corniche from his doorway, had called a greeting in Arabic to the guides and the older hustler had answered in English, calling back over his shoulder with a barked laugh: *ai, like a hambourger!*

Afterwards, in his hotel bed, he'd lain awake, humiliated, for most of the airless night and every shout and commotion in the back street below his window seemed to be the raised, impatient voices of his guides, waiting for him to slot neatly between them again in the morning. He had learned his one word of Arabic that evening, at the older guide's insistence: *Shukran*. Thank you. *Shukran*.

Since then he'd used silence more or less successfully in navigating the streets and souks of each city. In Marrakech he'd even found a source of hash without having to deal with the local sellers: a ravaged, middle-aged Frenchman called Pierre who seemed to be living year-round all alone on the shared balcony of a cheap hostel.

Still, he thought, conscious again of Ibrahim stirring beside him and relighting his sebsi, what was happening now wasn't so much a hustle as a kind of bargaining. If he wanted, he could simply fix a small price for a hike in the mountains. It would be just a hundred dirham, maybe, for the whole afternoon – easily affordable and probably worthwhile, especially if he got to see the huts where they processed the local hash. Pierre had told him that in the huts, when they beat the resin out of the plants, you could get high for free by breathing the thick golden dust that hung in the air. Yawning again, he fought the impulse to drop his head to his chest, sensing Ibrahim's watchful eyes on him.

Is it dangerous? he asked abruptly.

Alone, yes, of course. Alone, not permitted. But with me – not dangerous.

For a short while the boy considered the offer, but underneath his curiosity the prospect of Ibrahim's company all afternoon, of any company in fact, repulsed him. Just the effort of listening seemed to chafe at his brain. *Centougrade, Augoust, of coorse, pourmitted. Like a hambourger,* he recalled again, and felt the sweat come fresh to his face and scalp. He waited grimly for the bitterness to pass, listening to his tormentor puffing patiently at his *kif.* Well, this Ibrahim could go with him into the mountains if he wanted. It wasn't his problem if he expected to be paid at the end of it. It would be useful to get fresh water at the spring, and if some local bum insisted on keeping him company – fine. They needn't speak to each other. He hadn't hired him and he wouldn't pay, even if he had to give him the slip somehow. It was a strangely satisfying thought in fact and a new liveliness, a feeling of strength and self-righteous resolve, lifted the boy to his feet.

A good rest, said the voice at his side, as if to praise him. Ibrahim rose also and began immediately to climb the slope ahead of him, quick and sure-footed. Come. See the chapel, he called back. Very old. Many visitors.

The boy followed him slowly, up through the trees and out into the glare of the hilltop.

The ruin was roofless and in the main cavity of the building the remains of its white stone walls seemed to magnify the sun's heat from all sides. It's like a furnace in here, the boy said, more to himself than to Ibrahim. On his exposed forearms, pin-heads of white blisters were rising and prickling even as he watched, and when he rubbed them they flattened into smears of clear liquid. The boy looked around him. How old is this place?

Very old. Very old, said Ibrahim solemnly. First Mosque, centouries ago, then Spanish – *Católico* – then Mosque again, then ruin. See – the crosses. They are broken to make Mosque again. He pointed to one of the small, deep-set windows above their heads. It was clear that the arch had been bricked in at some point to form a cross, but at some later date again knocked through leaving just the extremities of the arms. Framed by the oddly shaped opening the hard, bright blue sky glittered like a gem.

The central tower of the Mosque was also ruined but its windows had not been blocked in; their shapely Muslim arches looked west towards the town, north and east to the tall, jagged Rif and south to the distant, hazy foothills of the Middle Atlas, rounded and blue-green. Without another word, Ibrahim disappeared inside the tower's crumbling narrow stairway. Emerging near the top he called the English boy up after him.

On the narrow balcony where the stairs opened out the boy took photographs of the town and the sharp grey horns of the Rif beyond, Ibrahim offering advice on the views and then, finally, pointing out the graveyard.

I walked up that way, the boy said.

Yes, said Ibrahim. Before, I stand here – he tapped the stone parapet in front of his stomach – and watch you walk there. Grinning, he made a walking motion with his fingers, then turned to climb back down the tower steps.

A qualm of distaste passed over the boy as he watched the narrow shoulders dropping from view. He imagined himself as he must have appeared from the vantage point of the tower, toiling up through the white stones and tussocks of grass like some tiny, noiseless insect. From the distant white bricolage of the town the long, faint cry of the midday call to prayer drifted up to him. It carried to the chapel in unpredictable fragments, the stretched, sombre phrases arriving or failing depending on the faint breeze. For a while he enjoyed the last of his solitude, then picked his way carefully down through the tower.

19

They left the chapel in single file, following a narrow path that wound steeply up towards the broken slopes of the nearest peaks. Here and there, stands of thorn and cacti hid rasping crickets, their dry clamour rising around the walkers like a protest as their feet crunched past. Soon, the boy was too parched and winded to speak even if he'd wanted to, and when Ibrahim stooped to gather up a handful of brittle herbs – good for the hort, he said earnestly, slapping his narrow chest – all the boy could do was nod, bow his head dutifully over the fistful of dusty stems and breathe in the pungent, eucalyptus scent. Very good for the hort, he repeated before scattering what he'd gathered and once more clambering on ahead.

After an hour or so they reached a tree – the first of any size since the slopes beneath the chapel – perched, incongruous, on a narrow terrace of rubble. Ibrahim waited in its shade for the boy to join him, then pointed out the deepest patch of shadow for him to rest in. Obediently, stunned by the high sun and the steepness of the climb, the boy sank down on the spot. When he closed his eyes tightly, squeezing the burning sweat from them, liquid lights writhed behind the lids. He reached out for the rough trunk of the tree to keep his balance.

Cooler here, he heard Ibrahim murmur, as if from behind a barrier of some kind that muffled the words. Good shade. A little water now, yes?

He drank to the last inch of fluid in the bottle, then offered it to Ibrahim, who refused with a smile and a shake of his head. Closing his eyes again the boy finished the water off and then leaned back uncomfortably against the tree's rough bark, still gasping from the climb. Even in the shade the air felt scorched. Each ragged breath seemed to parch his body further, as if he were being stripped of moisture from within. How long had he been exposed to this heat now? he wondered, dazed. It was at least four hours since he'd left his hostel and set off wandering through the quiet alleys and dead ends of the medina. He thought of the drinking fountains, their stone bowls painted white and powder blue, which he'd found from time to time on street corners and drunk greedily from. One of them had been jammed open and a band of small children had been splashing and laughing in the cool mud around the overflow. Everything about the water – the noisy spatter of it onto the packed dirt of the street, its cool touch on his bare legs, its almost salty limestone flavour – tormented him now.

Ibrahim was moving about under the tree. There was a rustle of dry leaves, the scrunch of footsteps on scree and then a tap on his forearm. The boy opened his eyes.

Taste, said Ibrahim, offering him a green pod. Carob, he said.

The tough husk was bitter and seemed to parch his mouth even more. He grimaced and spat the fragment away.

Not ready, Ibrahim agreed. Very…he made a puckering motion with his fingers in front of his mouth.

Sour, the boy said curtly.

Yes – soor. He flung away a second pod and stared wordlessly down the big, rock-strewn valley they had climbed up from. Very high, he said at last.

The boy nodded. To the side of the path a dry gulley had followed their course all the way from the chapel, its floor filled with a long, winding column of close-packed, pink flowers. For the first time now the boy stared over at them, curious. They seemed to grow without moisture or soil, not just in the gulley at hand but in every distant scar and parched streambed on the mountainsides round about them.

Wedding flowers, said Ibrahim, noticing his interest. He waved a hand towards the massed shrubs. When they come, it is the season to marry.

Oh, said the boy. Under the fleshy blossoms the dark, straight stems stood stiff and fairly tall – at least throat high – and grew as dense as maize. They would be easy to hide amongst.

Ibrahim said something in Arabic, naming them properly, the boy guessed.

You have a wife? asked Ibrahim.

The boy laughed. God, no – I'm too young for that. I'm just a student. He tossed away the bitten carob pod. It bounced high off a rock, like rubber. You? he asked.

Yes, a wife. I have five sons.

Five! How old?

The oldest – ten and four.

Fourteen?

Yes. Fourteen. The oldest.

The English boy looked again at the flowers. Their dark leaves and pale blossoms seemed oddly solid in the brightness and heat, like china, or enamel. How much farther to the spring now?

Not far now. Not even one hour. Rest more, yes? Ibrahim advised, and began filling his sebsi. When it was lit he offered it to the boy.

No. Mouth too dry, he mumbled.

Ibrahim nodded. Water soon. There, he said – pointing out a sharp stone ridge high above them and to the north.

That's where it is?

The spring, yes.

This spring – it never dries up, yes? It always has water?

Yes, yes. Summer, winter. Under the rocks – always water. He pointed to the flowers lining the gulley again. For the flowers, in the hot summer – always water. Allah provides, he announced.

There was silence for a while. Ibrahim smoked one pipeful, then lit another.

You guide many people up here?

Many visitors, yes. This year, not so many. Spanish, French, South African – still many. American, English – not so many. He streamed smoke through his nostrils. George Boosh, he said, and shrugged. To me, all visitors welcome.

The boy laughed. But Americans and English not quite so welcome?

Ibrahim laughed in return. To me, Americans, English, all welcome. My English – not so good. But very welcome, still. To me – yes. Always – *as-salam wa alaikum*, peace be upon you. Christian, Muslim – *as-salam wa alaikum*. Welcome.

Well, I'm not anything, the boy said.

Yes, not anything, Ibrahim repeated cheerfully. All welcome. He shrugged. Many visitors, they ask me to hire mules for journeys in the mountains. A thousand dirham every day. Sometimes, gifts too. All welcome. Two South Africans, a man and a wife, they come many years for seven days and nights in the mountains. The man, always photographing. The wife, always – he mimed writing, scribbling a ghost pencil over his palm. Many gifts from them, he finished.

The boy nodded and fell silent again while Ibrahim smoked. The mention of money and gifts was vexing, but now as he rested it fed his determination to be alone and at peace again. He glanced across at Ibrahim. His round, stony, close-cropped head was turned away towards the gulley. Okay, I'm ready, he announced, and eased himself upright. A cooler breath of wind was stirring – he could feel it on his face when he stood up though it was too gentle to move the compact leaves of the carob tree. Now that he was on his feet he could see the Spanish chapel again, white and tiny, its square tower like a stick of sugar or salt in the distance below them. They'd climbed a hell of a way, he thought – much higher than the mountain had seemed from its foot. And they still had almost as far again to go.

Ah! said Ibrahim, also noticing the breeze. Grinning at the boy, he spread his arms wide to embrace it. *Alhamdullillah*, he said. Thank God, yes? When there is a gift from God: *alhamdullillah*.

*Alhamdullillah*, the boy repeated dully.

Ibrahim nodded approvingly, then turned and left the shelter of the tree. Come, he said.

The boy had no idea how long they had been climbing before Ibrahim next stopped and led him, almost reeling with dizziness, into a narrow strip of shade. Very close now, very close, he could hear Ibrahim saying, but his mouth, even the deep connections in his brain, felt too clumsy and numb to master any words of his own.

Gradually, after what felt like many minutes, he realised they must be in the shade of the ridge they'd been aiming for. The path was nothing more than a goat track now, littered here and there with their smooth, pebble-like droppings, and the gulley with its long river of flowers was just a stumble away to the left, its sides almost sheer and its bed shrunk to a narrow cutting, though still packed tight with the tall, stubborn, pink-headed stems that had lined their long climb. Ibrahim was smoking again, but peering anxiously at him as he puffed his *kif*. Very close now. Five minutes, then water, very cool, he urged.

The boy shook his head. Listen, can you fill the bottle and bring me back some water? I need to rest. No more sun. He dug the empty water bottle out of his satchel and handed it to Ibrahim. The spring – it's just along the path, yes? Easy to find?

Yes – very easy. I come here many times for water. Many times. Always water here.

Okay, said the boy thickly. That's good. He rested his head on his knees, hiding his face. Already he felt a little stronger at the thought of escape.

He listened until the sound of Ibrahim's footsteps faded completely, then stood and checked that he was out of sight. Not far ahead, the track curved sharply around a bulge in the ridge. Quickly, his heart pounding, the boy scrambled down from the path into the steep-sided gulley. Within minutes he was buried deep amongst the stiff-stemmed, waxy-leaved flowers, ducking to keep his head below the level of the blossoms. The going was noisy and difficult – his feet slithered and twisted on jagged stones and the stems gave way reluctantly – but he forced himself to climb through the undergrowth for another hundred yards or so before stopping breathlessly. If Ibrahim searched for him, he would probably assume he was heading back down the mountain, the boy guessed, and anyway, from the point he had worked up to he could, if he needed to and if he dared, stand straight and get an overview of the path. Weakly he settled himself on a burning slab of rock and waited.

The flowers provided much less shade than he had imagined – the spearing sun was still too high to be blocked by the stems and leaves – and he cupped his hands around the back of his head. There was no sweat on his palms, he realised then, a ripple of nausea passing through him; they burned like cinders on the back of his neck, but both neck and palms were completely dry. He frowned and tried to swallow, feeling his throat grip unpleasantly on nothing.

The first shout was a much longer time coming than the boy had anticipated and, confusingly, there seemed no urgency or anger in it. The long, wavering call was calm – almost mournful – and weirdly penetrating, though he could make nothing of the words. It was like the call to prayer, he thought hazily, and remembered the narrow balcony of the tower again – Ibrahim's lookout – the bleached town and graveyard spread out below, and himself, watched from above, floundering up the slope, each movement tiny and ridiculous in the shimmering heat. Time after time, more times than he could keep count of in his exhausted daze, the long, wailing call rang out, sometimes nearer, sometimes farther.

Then, abruptly, it stopped, and when he struggled to his feet, swaying, all feeling gone from his legs, there was no sign of Ibrahim anywhere on the path. He forced his way out of the undergrowth with far more difficulty than he had entered, his head swimming now as he stumbled on the rocks underfoot, stiff leaves cutting across his hands and face. He paused to wretch but only a hot, bitter mouthful of clear fluid came. The final effort to clamber the steepest few yards back onto the track was beyond him at the first attempt, and as he slid helplessly backwards into the gulley he felt the first glimmerings of real horror at his vanished strength and coordination. It took a great effort of will not to call fearfully down the mountain after Ibrahim, and only the knowledge that the spring must be very close now persuaded him to rest on his knees, silently, and re-gather his energy instead.

Working more slowly and attacking the slope at an angle, he finally made the shade of the path, panting, almost sobbing with weakness and thirst. He would have to rest again, he realized, no matter how parched he was, and he slumped against the jagged wall of the ridge. When he closed his eyes he had the sensation of a giant oval pupil opening wetly at the back of his head, dilating and contracting with the rhythm of his pulse, black and glossy, and cool maybe, if he could just fall back a little, slip backwards into it, away from the pounding heat. If he opened his eyes, the ranks of flowers he had come from seemed to ripple and sway, though there was no wind to move them. They snaked away like a carpet of upturned faces, flat and naked to the sun.

Two days passed before Ibrahim was able to find more business at the chapel. A friendly, talkative young Dutch couple asked if they could hire him, very much wanting to see the view from the mountains and then to visit the cannabis farms. He had to speak English with them, which was tiring, but the girl spoke a little French, too, and even claimed to be learning Arabic. She had fallen in love with Chefchouen already, she said. She would like to learn Arabic and buy property there. It would be very cheap compared to Holland. Did the mountains around the town have names? she wanted to know.

Both the boy and girl had long, matted blond hair and they were dressed almost identically in loose cotton trousers and linen blouses. They held hands even in the worst of the heat, kissing and touching without embarrassment whenever they rested in the shade. When they were not whispering or caressing one another they were happy to share Ibrahim's *kif*, though the boy had a sebsi of his own which he passed sometimes to the girl. They could be twins, Ibrahim thought, watching them sidelong, amused and a little uncomfortable.

They found the body just beyond the tiny spring where they had stopped to rest and drink. For a moment Ibrahim was simply startled and angry at the thought of some other guide bringing tourists to his spring;

then he saw the boy's spoiled face and understood. He heard a loud, wordless shout, and realised it had come from his own mouth. Behind him, the girl too seemed to recognise suddenly what she was looking at and shrieked once, sharply. The English boy had come looking for the water and missed it, Ibrahim guessed at once, perhaps passing it again and again, not realizing that it was nothing more than a palm-sized, shallow pool hidden in the shadow of a flat rock. There was no running stream to give it away.

The boy's scorched forehead was open where he had collapsed onto a sharp stone and the blood had encouraged mountain dogs to take the eyes, ears and lips. A dark line of large, glossy ants was streaming in and out over the exposed white teeth. The ants were quick and purposeful, but here and there they reared up and wrestled where they collided, their long black forelegs rising and waving. They seemed like moving symbols when they stopped and jostled, as if a line of script had come evilly to life. Ibrahim suddenly recalled listening as a child to his grandfather's stories of the ruthless jinns of the mountains and a swelling panic began to knock his heart against his ribs. The ants could be the language of the jinn, he thought, and had to look away for a long moment before he could reassure himself that it was only the *kif* in his head making a child of him. The girl was at his side now, stooping and shaking one of the boy's stiff bare legs as if to try and wake him, moaning and babbling something – the same few words in her own unpleasant language – repeated over and over. Finally, the boyfriend took her free arm and pulled her roughly away.

Ibrahim was careful not to show any sign that he recognised the body, and he made sure that the Dutch couple, when they were calm enough to walk again, stayed with him to confirm his story when he reported to the authorities in the new quarter.

The police captain interviewed all three of them together, took written statements from the boy and girl and then interrogated Ibrahim alone. When they finally released him after the body had been examined on the mountain and a report radioed in, it was dark. The Dutch couple were gone and when he asked the guards on duty at the station door they laughed out loud and denied that either of the young foreigners had left the money they had agreed to pay him. What about the girl? Ibrahim insisted. Are you certain she left nothing? Not even an address? A message? They laughed again, insulted him, and pushed him out into the night.

He felt nothing more than annoyance at being cheated of his fee by the empty-headed Dutch boy, but walking towards his cousin's house at the foot of the medina where he planned to smoke and tell his story and sleep off the disastrous day, he felt strangely bitter towards the girl who had seemed friendly and had known a little Arabic and had asked him questions all the way up the mountain. It was foolish; an over-reaction, he knew. Allah provides. But still, he felt bitter. He would tell his cousin about the girl and about the ants, too. It had been like a dream, their streaming in and out of that ruined mouth. Why were they still in his mind, troubling him? He had the feeling that if he could speak about them it would be like brushing them away.

# DEAD OF WINTER

He'd had to park in Union Crescent, two long streets away, and now as he hurried towards home on foot, soaked and cursing, carrying the bodies of the two heavy pike in a straining plastic bag, the police loomed like sudden monuments out of the dark and swathes of rain. There were three of them at the street-level entrance to his tenement building, muttering and laughing, blocking the steps to his basement door. As he drew close he noticed that the ground floor flat above his own was cordoned off with yellow and black police tape. He stopped and waited for the figures in front of him to move. The three men were tall and motionless under the downpour. The water spattered heavy on their flat hats and streamed in rivulets down their bulky black nylon coats. Finally one took notice of him and shifted towards the road, letting him by. He felt their sudden silence at his back as he made his way down to the basement yard. Under the bridge of stone steps that connected the ground floor entrance to the street he paused, out of sight of the police and shielded from the rain. He shook himself and loosened his clothes where the wet had plastered them to his skin. The yard smelled like old bread under the span of the arch and the damp, sheltered air was filled with tiny grey gnats. He waved a hand in front of his face where they had already begun to congregate. For a short time then he stood still and strained to hear what the police above him were talking about, but the spit and hiss of the rain drowned out everything other than one more low purl of laughter.

Inside, the kitchen strip light was already on. He kicked off his wet shoes and crossed the tiles to the cooker. A small covered pan sat cold on the hob and when he lifted the lid he saw it was half full of congealed baked beans. A strong, caramel-like sweetness bloomed up from them. He put the lid back on and hefted the bag of pike up onto the steel draining board next to the hob. The two fish, stiff and curved, slid with a rush under their own dead weight through the plastic neck of the bag onto the metal. A gout of clear, stringy fluid spilled after them. They were each between four and five pounds – good solid pike though their colour was already spoiled. He considered cleaning them there and then but decided it could wait until he'd dried and changed. Leaving the water and slime to drain, he opened the door to the living room and looked in.

Karen was slumped on the sofa, asleep in front of the TV. A thin downie covered her up to the chin. Her head was fallen to one side and her mouth hung open. The downie cover was patterned with big prints of washed-out blue roses. A hungry weariness washed over him. He peeled off his sodden jumper and draped it over a kitchen chair, then went back to the living room. The TV was still on, the volume turned low. He crossed the room and turned it off. The sound of the rain washed in, whispering and spluttering. Karen closed and opened her mouth, making a tacky chewing noise, then opened her eyes.

Malcolm, she said thickly, what time is it?

Not late, he said.

She yawned and thought for a moment. I left some food for you.

I know, he said. He scratched the back of his neck, staring at a point somewhere to the side of her. Thanks.

Did you catch anything? You didn't bring anything back, did you?

Only two.

She groaned. Why do you have to bring them back? They taste terrible. No one else I know ever had to eat a pike.

They taste fine. It's just the bones you don't like.

Oh Christ. Don't even talk about the bones.

He shrugged. I'll eat them myself. You don't have to eat them.

She grimaced. Why don't you just put them back, Mal, like everyone else? Just because you catch something doesn't mean you have to kill it. She sighed and lolled her head. What kind of fun is it anyway, fishing that horrible little loch in the dead of winter? More wakeful now, she looked him up and down. You're soaking, she said. It was so sunny this morning.

Aye. It came on with the dark. He tilted his head from side to side, stretching the tight muscles. What's the polis doing out there?

God yes, she said, sleeping made me forget! God Mal, you won't believe it – the old wifie above us got killed. They questioned me and everything.

Killed?

Murdered. I couldn't believe it. Right over this room. She stared wide-eyed at him. It really spooked me, Mal. What if –

Christ, they don't want you for a witness, do they?

No, no. I heard some banging and thumping but I didn't tell them. They'd already caught who did it – two kids broke in and they were still there when the police came. Someone in the block opposite saw them getting in and phoned.

Malcolm shook his head, looking at the blank screen on the TV. He could feel Karen staring at him and remembered the police muttering and laughing in the street outside. He started cracking his fingers. So they beat her up? he said abruptly.

With bits of furniture, I think. It was horrible. Mal, don't crack your fingers, she said.

I doubt if they meant to kill her. Probably she started shouting.

Well they killed her alright. Anyway Mal, don't be like that.

Like what?

She didn't answer.

I'll get changed and have something to eat, he said at last.


Without looking at the two cold, glazed pike at his elbow he heated the beans quickly, the sauce breaking into rapid, dull bubbles. He stirred them up and left them on a low heat while he grilled and buttered some toast. The beans, softened by standing and reheating, poured like slurry over the bread. He filled the pan with cold water and let it soak while he ate.

Once he'd finished eating he looked in the fridge and found a can of Guinness. Back in the living room the TV was on again. Montel was reasoning with somebody.

Karen looked up at him furtively and he knew what was coming. Can you see if I've got any ciggies left – I'm hiding them in the cupboard so I don't get tempted too much.

31

He checked the sideboard cupboard and took out a half full pack of Silk Cut. You shouldn't smoke at all, the way you are.

I *know*, she said, mock-wounded. I've only had two all day though.

He tossed them to her.

She smiled at him and held a hand out towards his drink. He passed the can over, closed the door behind him and sat on the sofa next to her. She took a few long, thirsty swallows. He took the can back.

She's been moving a lot today, she said, and smiled again at him.

He nodded. Good, he said.

Feel, she said.

No, no. I believe you. It's moving.

*Feel*, she insisted.

He slipped a hand between the buttons on her dress and laid the palm flat on her taut stomach. It felt hot. He waited.

Wait for it, she said.

He left his hand there, glancing over at the TV. The news was running – more war somewhere; old women crying in some cold Balkan town. They looked like gypsies, he thought.

There! she said.

Something pressed, then seemed to writhe across the flat of his hand. He jerked his arm back.

Did you feel it?

A kick, he said.

She pulled the downie back up.

He took a long drink. He held the black, sour liquid in his mouth until it warmed into froth, then swallowed.

Give me your hand back, she said.

No. Leave it now.

Go on. Please, she murmured. Put the can down, Mal.

He placed the can on the floor and let her take his hand. She warmed it between her palms then guided it under the downie to rest on her thighs. He felt her hitch her dress shorter, inch by inch, then felt her hand on his again, urging his fingers onto the heat between her open legs. She was damp through the cotton of her pants and for a while he pressed and circled gently there without slipping inside them. Then finally he eased his way under the gusset and brought her quickly to a sharp, juddering orgasm, stopping only when she snatched his hand away, half giggling, half shrieking when he pretended to resist her.

Oh Christ! she gasped, and went on laughing almost soundlessly. It's so easy to come when I'm this big. She took a deep breath. It must all be the pressure down there or something. I get so horny some days, too.

He smiled and drew his hand back.

God, she whispered, and rolled her head, eyes shut.

He reached for his drink again and watched the rest of the news. By now the local reports were on and he realised the pictures were of the street outside and the dead woman's flat. The sound was too low to hear the commentary, but they were interviewing someone half familiar, maybe a neighbour. The day had still been dry then, Malcolm noted. In the background the sun was flashing on the tenement windows.

Why does everyone love murders? Karen mumbled.

I thought you were sleeping.

She shook her head. Every afternoon they put on Columbo and Quincey, and on the news it's always this kind of thing. And now it's our street. Why does everyone want to see it? Then she smirked at him. I'm still tingling though, she said drowsily. But I shouldn't have had that Guinness – it's repeating now. I feel like that fairy-tale wolf sewn up full of stones.

Guinness is good for you.

Uh huh. She belched loudly and they both laughed. Then she closed her eyes again.

Malcolm looked down at the can clasped on his lap. Karen's scent was strong on his fingers; a heavy, bacterial perfume, much more pungent, he thought, than it had been before she fell pregnant. He closed his eyes, fighting back a familiar rolling black wave of unhappiness, and found himself thinking about the generations that must have lived out their time and died in the building around him, in the dark stone layers of tenement flats above, through centuries, layer on layer of births and lives and deaths. The stone steps to the murdered woman's flat and to their own were worn smooth and cupped. How many lives to do that? How many dead feet? Brooding, he remembered the two pike, cold and smooth as enamel, and then his mind went back to the small, deep, peat-blackened loch he'd fished through the day. As the dusk and first drops of rain had come on a third fish had run with his bait; two heavy, jarring knocks and then clean away. A big fish, he instinctively knew; as big or bigger maybe than anything he'd caught before. He knew the loch hid monsters. One autumn evening, fishing it from his brother's small, fibreglass dinghy, he'd hooked something on a deadbait that for five minutes or more towed the boat in a slow, deliberate circle round its anchor. He remembered the feeling in his arms and shoulders as he'd tried to wear out its terrible, lazy strength. He'd been almost glad when the trace snapped.

The fish he'd hooked today was nowhere near as monstrous. Though he supposed there was no way of knowing for sure – it had thrown the bait so quickly. Just two sickening arm and heart-wrenching thumps and then gone; back to the big stones and weed forests of the bottom; lost to him forever, probably. It occurred to him that as a boy he'd taken the loss of such fish badly, as a kind of bereavement even, which could wake and torment him at night with frustration and sorrow; now, the thought of failing to draw something so heavy and secret out of the loch brought him a morbid, premonitory sense of relief. What fun is it? she'd asked. And she was right – it was something, but not pleasure. Not that at all.

Mal, what's wrong?

He turned to her, startled. Nothing, he said. He got up and stretched, glad to move his tight chest. He picked up the remote and switched channels on the TV, finding what was left of a film and then watching it, still standing. Suddenly he looked up from the screen. Christ it's dark in here, he said. He reached over to the dimmer switch on the wall near the door and turned the lights right up.

Don't Mal. You can see the lights on the screen. Turn it back.

He looked at the screen and saw it was true; the lights made ghost-lamps on the screen. He turned the switch back again and the reflections faded to pinpoints.

Now I know where they are I can't take my eyes off them, she complained.

He didn't know the film but there were plenty of half-familiar faces in it. He started trying to remember what other parts he'd seen the actors playing. The film was some sort of detective story with a priest in it. Mainly he wondered what else he remembered the priest as. Something in uniform, he guessed.

We ought to get a dog, he said.

She looked at him, surprised. Not a dog. I'd rather a cat. I love cats.

Not for a pet, he said. He belched quietly, holding his chest. I mean for protection. To warn you.

Cats can warn you too, with sixth sense, she said.

He shook his head. A cat's no good, he said. What use is a fucking cat?

A cat could eat all the filthy fish you bring home. Anyway, I thought you'd like a cat. You're a bit of a tomcat yourself, aren't you? With your fish. Like a big daft cat dropping dead stuff on the doorstep. She reached out from under the downie to prod his ribs. Aren't you? she teased.

He realised he didn't want to talk anymore. He felt tired, and thought of the rain drumming onto his head and back, heavy and steady like it might never stop. I'm going to bed, he told her.

I'll come too, she said. I'm tired too.

He turned the TV off, then made his way through the kitchen to the bathroom.

She got up, pushing herself straight. She heard the bathroom door close and the bolt slot into place.

Lock up, he called out to her from behind the door. Both locks.

Carrying her cigarettes she walked into the dark kitchen and flicked on the light. Outside, the rain sounded heavier than ever. She took a cigarette and lit it from the hob. She turned to the pike resting on the steel drainer and inspected them, running a fingertip lightly over one of the smooth dry eyes. There was no sound of movement from the bathroom. She paused, then padded to the front door and opened it.

From the doorstep she looked up to the street above and saw the police cars had all gone. The night was quiet except for the rain. There was no traffic; no footsteps or voices. It was pleasant to stand there, listening and smoking. Beyond the step most of the sunken yard was awash now.

Suddenly her right eye pricked and blurred and as she blinked she felt something give under the wet lid. She cleared her eye and looked up again and noticed the gnats, a cloud of them lifting and falling in the brightness streaming out from the kitchen at her back. She watched them and up above, through the downpour, a car sped past, its wet tyres making a sound like leaves soughing in the wind. For a little while she tried to remember the last time she'd seen the old woman from the flat above. Maybe crossing the road with a small dog. Did she have a dog, though? She couldn't really remember. Maybe that was a different old woman. She swept something, another gnat, out of the hair above her eyes, then brushed at her face as it fell. She wondered at them coming so near – in the day her cigarettes always kept them at a distance. They were certainly getting close now though, drawn to the light, she guessed. In the yard itself her old cigarette ends were swimming around the flooded slabs close to her feet. The rainwater had welled them up from the drain where she'd dropped them and there were four of them butting against the raised grill like little tied boats. Others drifted in the opposite corner of the yard, just under the surface, soft and fat, making big, lazy circles. She took a long, deep draw, then let the smoke go slowly. Another gnat whined in her ear, making her flinch, and in disgust she dropped her cigarette and lashed at them, one arm cradling her stomach. She felt tiny forms hit and stick to her palm. She reached out again, further, straining forward into space.

# EVERYWHERE WAS WATER ONCE

I saw them coming down the old mountain road at noon. I was looking out the little side window of the hotel kitchen, cutting radishes into claw shapes for the salad. Just behind me, Luke was hacking through bones, thumping his favourite old cleaver into the chopping board, swinging so hard the steel worktop under the board boomed and rang like the metal was taking the hits: *bang! bang! bang!*

They came slowly down the road, one tall, one much shorter and heavier built. They both carried big back-packs and stooped under the weight of them. It was a hot day, hot as any that summer, and they looked like they'd been walking a long time in the heat. The shorter one stopped just as they reached the school at the edge of the village. He bent himself nearly double and shucked his pack forward towards his shoulders, then tightened the straps. The tall one waited, staring into the village. They both stood there a while, talking, just beyond the long, shady tunnel of trees that stops where the mountain road ends and the High Street begins.

Luke tapped my shoulder and handed me a fresh rabbit's foot. Hang it in the sun, he said, and don't let it get wet. Wet'll make it rot.

I turned it over in my hand. Soft, like something for a baby.

It's a luck-charm, he said.

I put it in the big front pocket of my waitressing apron. When I looked again, the walkers were gone.

It was early afternoon when they came into the bar. I was clearing the dessert plates for old Pastor Williams and his sister. The two walkers dumped their rucksacks by the door and took a good look around. The shorter one, a fair-haired boy not much older than me, I guessed, was red in the face and sweating. His tall, darker friend looked easy with the heat, and calm. He walked to the bar while his friend took a seat in the shade. I put the dirty plates down on an empty table and hurried to get behind the bar before Mr Whitfield came through.

The stranger smiled, but not enough to show his teeth. Two bottles from the fridge, he said, pointing. Beer, please.

He sounded foreign and I felt my mouth go dry. Budweiser? I said.

Anything, he said.

In bottles we've got Budweiser or Heineken.

Either.

I could feel old Williams watching me but served the drinks anyway and took the money. When I went back for the dirty plates he said: Sarah fach, you leave that kind of work to Mr Whitfield, now. He looked from one stranger to the other, then back again to me.

He's not here, I said in Welsh, feeling my face burn.

He carried on in English. There's Luke back in the kitchen there, he said.

The tall one was staring at Mr Williams now, but still smiling the same smile. Then Mr Whitfield came up from the cellar anyway and nothing else was said.

I took the plates through to the kitchen and when I came back to the bar the younger stranger was looking at the blackboard near the door. It said 'Today's Special – Trout Fresh From The Lake'. I'd written it out neat that morning, in yellow chalk. They spoke quietly and the tall one went up to the bar.

Thanking you sir, said Mr Whitfield after taking his order. Then he waved me over.

Tell Luke he's back on, he said under his breath, and tell him no pissing and moaning.

I went out through the kitchen and started up the fire escape to Luke's room. He must have heard me clunking up the metal steps because before I got to the top he was out on his little platform looking down. All he had on were white underpants. I stopped. The metal was burning in the sun and he hopped from foot to bare foot.

No way, he said, before I could speak.

He says you've got to. There's two late customers.

Ah! Ah! he said, still hopping. Tell him to kiss my arse. I laughed. Okay, I said, and turned to go down.

My fucking feet! he yelled. I looked back but he'd disappeared.

In the kitchen I took down the big pan, got the lettuce bowl and trout out of the cabinet fridge and arranged it all ready for him.

Back in the bar Mr Whitfield was sitting with Mr and Mrs Williams, talking lambs in Welsh. It had been a terrible spring and dozens froze in the fields. Now, this early summer was the hottest anyone could remember.

You can't question, though, I heard Mr Williams say in his throaty old preaching voice.

No, you can't question, said his sister, wobbling her head.

I noticed that the two strangers were watching them talk. They'd finished their first drinks and had two fresh bottles in front of them.

I found a few things to do at the bar. I emptied the slop trays and shuffled some bottles. Now and again I looked over at the strangers, sideways on. The tall one caught me every time. There he was, smiling like he knew something. Soon I heard Luke clattering pans in the kitchen, which is what he does when he wants me through there to help him. I went through fast before he broke anything.

Luke was still in his underpants. He'd put on shoes but that was all.

That's not hygienic, I said.

They're clean.

They weren't. I went over to the fridge and got out a mini-trifle. I found a spoon on the draining board and ate the trifle fast, watching Luke work.

He picked up the trout from the chopping board. You can smell that shitty lake in these things, he said. You can taste it when you eat them. You can taste the silt. He laid the fish in a pan of hot butter and tossed some mushrooms and chopped bacon and sliced almonds in with it. Put out the salad, he said.

I rinsed out the metal trifle dish, then got the salad ready. I threw in some extra green to use it up, all round the plate, then set it down next to Luke.

Jesus, I said a salad, not a garden. He lifted the trout onto it, then scooped the mushrooms, bacon and a few greasy almond slivers over the top. He cut a wedge of lemon and rustled it into the lettuce and cress.

It was quiet back in the bar but I could feel the bad atmosphere. Mr Whitfield was staring at the two walkers. The younger boy was looking down at his feet. Mr Williams shook his head, though I couldn't tell why. I walked on over and put the plate in front of the tall one.

It's not for me, he said, and pushed it in front of the boy. Any vinegar? he asked.

I went to fetch it from the bar and when I handed him the glass drizzler he took the stopper right out and splashed vinegar all over the boy's fish, drenching it, washing the almonds off. I almost laughed with surprise, imagining what Luke would say, but the boy just watched, showing no emotion at all.

Back in the kitchen there was no sign of Luke and Mr Whitfield stayed put in the bar, watching the strangers, probably. The kitchen was hotter than the bar and I had a terrible thirst. I ate another trifle and drank cold water from the tap before going in to clear their table.

The bar was empty. I went to the window, quickly, and looked out onto the street. The air smelled of dust and tar. I leaned out and in the distance there was Mr Williams, stooping and slow, helping his sister up the road. Then a big heavy hand squeezed hard behind and in-between and I nearly jumped out into the street.

Tidy up after them grubby hippies, there's my girl, Mr Whitfield said.

Get off me, I shouted, and slapped at his hand.

He let go but I could still feel the throb where his big filthy fingers had been.

Be grateful someone gives you a bit of attention, he said. Then he went back behind the bar and started going through the till.

The boy had finished off almost all the fish, but he hadn't touched the salad. The skeleton was left there, in the middle of it all. There was vinegar pooled all round the rim. I picked up the plate, careful not to spill, and carried it through.

After washing up I hung my apron behind the door. There was a dark brown stain, just a spot, on the front pocket and I wondered for a second until I remembered the rabbit's foot. I fished it out to see – there was a little black knob of blood crusted on the tip of the bone. I wrapped it in foil so Luke wouldn't find it, then buried it down with the rubbish.

Somehow I knew where I'd find the two walkers when I got out. I could feel it. I ran across the road and along to the wicket gate that gives onto the fields around the lake. Near the water the fields stop dead and drop just a foot or so down to stones and mud, like a step or a bench, and they were sitting on it, down along the shore in the distance. Thin milky clouds had come over and taken the glare from the sun, but that just made the hot air seem trapped and suffocating. I was breathing hard and trying not to swallow the tiny grey flies coming off the muddy shore like puffs of smoke. The further on I went the thicker the gnats seemed to swarm, sticking to my sweating face, tangling in my hair.

Just a short way down from the strangers a man was fishing for trout. He'd waded in up to his waist and the two boys were watching him. The water was as still as I'd ever seen it. Even when the fisherman moved to cast the ripples seemed wrong – they started to flow out, but then just flattened back into the surface. As I got close I tried to look surprised, as if I'd chanced on them. The tall one smiled and waved me over. It was a big smile this time, showing off his crooked teeth. I could smell dope in the air, and the younger boy's eyes were nearly as glassy as the lake. I sat close to the tall one.

I remember your name, he said.

It seemed like a funny thing to say. I laughed a bit, to cover up my nerves. He was staring at me. What was he? I wondered. Some kind of European. His skin was olive and his long hair was straight and very black. Maybe a gypsy, I thought.

We just skinned up, he said. Stay if you want.

I nodded and looked over at the fisherman. I wondered if I knew him, and if he knew me. I couldn't tell from where I was sitting. He had a straw hat on and sunglasses. Anyway, I thought, he isn't watching.

I'd smoked dope once before, in Luke's room, and I'd lain there and watched Luke himself smoking plenty of times so I wasn't too nervous. I didn't want to cough though, so I just took a gentle nip when he offered it to me, then drew it down really careful and passed it on to the boy. He took it and really sucked at it, heaving the smoke right down. The tall one and me both laughed. When I got hold of it again I took a better draw and coughed a bit, but that was okay now.

I didn't notice the fisherman going. I just looked up at some point and he was gone and there was the lake, huge and still and empty from end to end.

What do you do at night? I asked. I was hoping he'd want me to find them a place to stay. I was thinking I could get them into Gran's by the back door and then up to my room. Gran was bedridden downstairs and was going deaf and had the radio going loud till all hours so I doubted she'd hear them.

He shrugged.

Do you need somewhere? I looked at him and tried to smile.

We know where we're sleeping tonight, he said. Then he lay back, his long legs still hanging over the edge of the field. He closed his eyes.

The younger boy was finishing off the joint, staring out across the lake.

I looked back down at the other's face. There was a cloud of flies over it – big, long-bodied black ones now, not the little grey gnats I'd walked through. Some had landed and one was walking slowly along his bottom lip, like it was looking for an opening. He didn't seem to feel them, or he didn't mind. It gave me a strange, light-headed feeling. I waved them off, then got up and walked down to the water. All along the margin there was a rim of green slime. I poked around at it with the toe of my shoe and a smell of rot and sewage started to come up off it, so I stopped. Just out from the shore, a few inches underwater, lay a dead perch. It was half in and half out of the soft grey silt that's under all the lake. The perch's mouth was open and the mud had washed right in. It looked like all the foul mud in the lake had spilled out from its mouth. I remembered what Luke had said about tasting silt in the trout.

I looked round at the two strangers. They were both lying flat out now. I started off back along the shore. I turned a few times, but they didn't see me go.

I worked the bar with Mr Whitfield that evening because Gwen, his regular, was off on holiday. It was quiet but Mr Whitfield kept his hands to himself for once. He reckoned he had a migraine and was sickening for something. I got out late, around twelve, because Mr Whitfield couldn't help with clearing up. He started doing the Gents and threw up twice into the washbasin. After that he sat by an open window and let me get on with it. He even let me do the till.

By the time I was leaving he said he felt better, though his face was frightening: much older seeming; waxy and grey. I stayed on the pavement and listened to him lock up inside, then watched for the lights going off downstairs and going on in his flat above. Then I went round the side and looked up the fire escape at Luke's place, but everything was dark. I started off for home, wondering if Gran would be awake and fussing.

It was much cooler now and I knew the weather was turning. A wind was picking up and blowing in off the lake. I could hear sheep-calls from the fields near the water, carried in on the breeze. They were calling from all around the lake. There were distant ones, coming in faint from the far shore. It seemed to get under my skin and make me restless too, wide awake and waiting for something. I felt like I needed to keep walking, like I could walk forever through the night, never sleeping, listening and smelling the air like an animal.

I came to the statue where the road forks and that was where I heard their voices. At first I just stood still, straining to listen. They were somewhere on the triangle of grass behind the monument. There were hedges all round the lawn, hiding them. I stepped out onto the road and squeezed through where the hedge butts up against the statue. Rubbing against the cold stone plinth and seeing the lifted bronze arm and book up above me I suddenly got scared, and was just about to sneak back to the road when the tall one called my name. Sarah, he said, and I saw them, laid out side by side on the grass.

Who's the statue of? he asked.

All I could make out were their two dark sleeping bags, big and coffin-shaped. I could hardly speak. I don't know, I said. I did know, but that was what I said.

He sat up and I heard the flint on his lighter scrape, but it didn't catch. He tried again and suddenly I could see his face behind the little blue flame. He lit a long thin joint. Have a smoke, he said, so I sat between them and took a draw each time I was offered it.

I don't know how long I sat there smoking. When the first joint ended he rolled up another, and another after that. For a long while they hardly said a word, then they started talking, softly, as if I wasn't there, about where they'd been, where they planned to go. I had the last of a joint to myself by then and it was making me strange, and while they talked I had the feeling of having known all the place-names they were murmuring, even places I'd never heard of, and I missed them, like I was homesick for everywhere. I had a picture in my mind then of Luke's room, of this pair of baby-shoes he had nailed over his bed with *Go Faster!* written under them, and the fossil he kept on his bedside table, a big stone sea-shell he found high up on the mountain.

I must have fallen into a dream soon after because the next thing I remember is realising that the tall one was asleep and the boy was sat up, turned to me, quiet as death. I was cold, and the wind was getting stronger, shaking the high privet hedge round about us. The wind was carrying the silt-smell off the lake. I remembered the dead perch and thought about the waves slapping on the shore now, stirring it all up, all the rotted things that were settled there. The waves are like mouths, I thought, eating up everything in the end, eating up the land. I remembered again about Luke and the tiny shoes over his bed, and the fossil. I knew it was all connected, but didn't know how, except that everything was silt, or if it wasn't it would be, and everywhere was water once, and would be again.

I touched the tall one's face and it was hot and smooth and dry. His eyes flicked open.

Let me in, I said.

He was nude under the covering, and really there wasn't room for us both, but I kept my hands from touching him. My father's gone and my mother's dead, I told him, and he nodded, like he'd always known.

We lay still for a while, pressed together but flat on our backs. The wind had cleared the sky again and all the starfields were bright and deep. He pointed up to one of the clusters. See there? he said. The Great Bear.

I looked along the line of his arm and finger. I don't see it, I said. Nothing looks like a bear.

There, he said, tracing a shape. There's the tail, high up, and his head down low. See it now? It points that way in summer, like he's sniffing his way down.

I laughed. None of it looks like anything, I said, and remembered something Luke told me once when he was very drunk, before we'd ever done anything together. He'd told me that when he was a boy he used to sneak into the garden at night and pray to the brightest stars, imagining they were spaceships and their captains could read his thoughts. What did you ask for? I'd wanted to know, but then we both just fell about laughing and he never talked about it again. Now, I pictured all the clutter in his room, fossils, driftwood and bones, all the random things he found meanings in, and I pictured the rabbit's foot, as if I'd kept it, hung on a wire in the sun.

The stranger turned to face me and rested a burning hand on my leg. I forced the tight band of my work skirt over my hips and when it reached his fingers he helped me push it right off. He waited, watching my face, then touched me through my pants, making me gasp. I lifted myself and he rolled them down to my feet. Then he waited again, brushing my forehead with smooth, papery lips. They were parted, but I couldn't feel his breath. Behind us, the boy sniffed quietly like a dog, and I thought of Luke again, kneeling in the dark.

Come inside me, I said. And for a while, the boy watching us without a word, the stranger set himself on top of me, heavy and hot, and filled me so full I couldn't speak, could hardly breathe, and couldn't stop crying.

Hush, he whispered as he pushed, hush.

Afterwards, he rolled away and seemed to sleep again. I lay there a long time, close against him, my head to the ground, listening, feeling his liquid come back out of me, warm but soon cold like any other kind of water. It seemed like the whole world was sleeping and in the silence under the stars, under the Great Bear creeping down, I could hear everything, even the quietest things. I can hear the worms, I said. I can hear the worms moving through the earth.

# SALMON

The dog appeared just as the last of the voices faded away – a black, hungry-looking lurcher. It stood motionless at the lip of the tall riverbank, staring down across the cold quick water at him. A faint call came from someone in the family of walkers he'd heard tramping and chattering somewhere out of sight, above him on the opposite side. The dog quivered, yelped, then twisted away and back into the hidden fields of rough pasture behind it. He shrugged his pack higher on his shoulders and strode on. After just a few steps the dog burst back into view again, scraping to a halt just inches from the high, undercut brink. This time it ignored the distant calls and whistles, staying to watch him labouring under his pack and fishing tackle until he had long passed it and was out of sight around the wide sweep of the river bend.

He finally made the road bridge at noon, sweating and fly-ridden. He clambered wearily up to it from the river's edge and was glad to rest there. The sun was punishing on his bare neck and head and inside his boots his hot feet were soft and swollen, soaked with sweat and blister-water. He rested his rod against the stone parapet of the bridge, struggled out of his pack and creel and leaned back on the low stone wall, his arms splayed to support him. After a while he stooped down and worked a plastic water bottle out of a side pocket of his pack, drank from it and then poured some of the water over his head. It felt warm, like the fluid in his boots, he imagined, and the smell of hot tarmac from the road mingled queasily in his nose and throat with the plastic scent of the water from the bottle. He twisted the top back on and re-packed it.

Turning away from the road, he leaned to look over the parapet into the river. He knew the bigger trout would be aligned just under the arch, out of sight, behind the shadow-line, but he could see the occasional glint upstream of the younger, smaller fish as they turned to take food under the rippled surface, then as they turned again to find their lies in the open river, out in the full glare of the sun. He wished he'd had the sense to stay near the bridge to fish, pitching the tent after dark maybe, instead of walking so far upriver to the quieter stretches. He would have had plenty of chances under the bridge, even in this weather.

There was still another half-hour or so of walking before reaching the town, he guessed. He hoisted the rucksack up onto the lip of the parapet, tilting its weight from there onto his shoulders, then hooking his arms through its straps and moving forward to take the strain. The fishing rod and creel he carried first in one hand, then the other, using the tip of the cotton rod-bag to flick the sweat and flies away from his eyes and lips.

As he walked through the main street the little town seemed deserted. For a while he didn't even see any traffic, then a loud, battered dirt-bike raced past him from behind, turned at the head of the street and passed him again. The skinny, T-shirted boy riding it stared full into his face as he sped past.

At the empty bus-stop he set down his fishing gear and slid the pack from his shoulders. The long street, sweeping in a gentle curve down and away from him, seemed to channel a faint breeze and he turned his back to it, letting it cool the aching wetness along his spine. At last a few cars sped past, and a small white camper slowed and parked outside the post office some fifty yards down the street. A cafe was open just a few doors along from the bus-stop and leaving his gear he walked stiffly down to it.

The cafe was surprisingly cool inside. A girl in a dirty blue apron was wiping down a big steel tea-urn behind the counter.

Have you got any cold Coke? he asked.

In the fridge, there.

He looked around for the fridge, finding it just behind his back, half hidden by the open door of the cafe. The girl finished cleaning the urn before serving him, then took the money in a hand still damp from the rag she'd been using.

Back outside he saw that a small, ferrety-looking man had taken a seat at the bus-stop and was eyeing the fishing gear. The fisherman watched him from the door of the cafe, drinking his Coke in the shade, taking big, painful gulps that were hard to keep down. He drained the can quickly, then dropped it into a mesh waste-basket at the side of the café door. He belched, and a little Coke welled up, still cold.

As he approached, the new arrival looked up from examining the pack and fishing tackle and nodded. The fisherman nodded back.

Yours then, aye? Nice to find a bit of time for the fishing, like. He peeled the cardboard lid off from a small tub of ice-cream and licked the inside of it clean. He twitched his narrow head, glanced around and then went on talking, nervily. Eh, Jesus, I'll be glad to get on home, meself. Been working from three this morning, me. He had a reedy, Geordie voice and nodded his head continuously down to one side, deferentially, as he spoke. The sharp chin and jaw lines of his boyish face were peppered with a gingery stubble. The stubble didn't match his thinning hair, which was watery brown, like his eyes. He grinned shyly at the fisherman.

A long day, said the fisherman.

All paid nicely for, mind. Aye, all paid nicely for, he said again, and looked set to go on talking, but first he spooned a soft pat of ice-cream into his mouth with a little plastic paddle. I'll be glad to get home mind, he said after swallowing. Glad to get to bed, like.

The fisherman nodded. Know when the bus is due?

The man spooned in another lump of ice-cream, this time talking through it. Naw. Normal days I get me a lift home from the slaughterhouse like, so I don't pay any attention to the buses.

The slaughterhouse? he said, interested.

Aye. A tear of ice-cream welled at the corner of his mouth and started to trickle. He smeared it with the back of his hand.

What's it you do there then?

The man cleared his throat. I'm on the tripe bags, me. Mind I can do the guts too.

The fisherman looked more closely at the crusty brown specks he'd already noticed sprinkling the collar at the front of the man's white

T-shirt. Is it cows you do?

Aye, cows and lambs. And the odd run of pigs, like. Mainly lambs now mind, this time of year. Two thousand through today. That's how I was in early like. Lots of money to be made with the overtime this week, like.

There were more tiny stains, the fisherman noticed now, some on the side of his chin and one, darker and smoother, along his right ear lobe.

The slaughterman started scraping at the last of the ice-cream but it was too far gone in the heat. He gave up and drank the remains straight from the tub.

The fisherman looked at his watch and sighed. Christ, it's hot, he said.

Aye, the slaughterman agreed.

The fisherman tipped his pack and sat on it, levelling his legs out onto the road. Must be a hell of a job in this heat, he said.

The slaughterman blinked at him, surprised. Naw, he said mildly, and shook his head. Naw, it's fantastic, a great laugh with all the lads, like. He placed the empty ice-cream tub at his feet, then straightened back up. The fisherman glanced from the empty tub to the man's boots, filthy with dried blood. They were big and steel toe-capped; yellow, like big, dangerous clowns' boots. A great job, he went on. They're great lads, like. And I can get a whole lamb for the mother for thirty quid, me. Thirty quid! And I *know* it's been killed fresh the day. Oh aye. Aye, it's great. He fumbled in a pocket and found a pack of Embassy blues. He offered one to the fisherman, who shook his head. The slaughterman lit up and drew down hard, then breathed it back contentedly. Thirty or forty depending on size, like, he said.

Behind them the door of a hotel snapped shut and they both turned. A heavy, red-faced man strolled over to them. He stopped between them and looked from one to the other, appraisingly. In the end he addressed himself to the fisherman.

Still no fucking bus eh? I've been watching from that window there since five o' fucking clock. Another public transport fuck-up, eh? Why do we fucking bother? Eh? He stared down at the fisherman, then at the fishing tackle. He worked his top lip from the inside with his tongue and the thick brown clump of his moustache shrugged and bristled. His tongue found something and scooped it back and he took his time mashing it with his front teeth. Five past fucking five, eh?

The fisherman nodded and stood up, uneasy with the big stranger looming over him.

Been fishing, eh pal? He picked up the rod and felt for the sections inside the cotton bag, gauging them with his fingertips. Is it for trout this is for then? He belched massively and the fisherman caught a strong, stale waft of beer.

The fisherman nodded, watching the man's thick fingers stumbling over the slim tubes under the cloth.

Must be, eh? He was addressing the slaughterman now, suddenly. Too fucking dinky for salmon, this rig. He snorted. Aye by Christ. He looked away across the road. Up in the hills? He tilted the rod to a wide gap between a garage and a church on the opposite side of the wide street. Through it the border hills were visible, rolling back into the pale late afternoon haze. The fisherman nodded, and the big man turned back to the slaughterhouse worker. You too, pal?

Naw. He grinned, embarrassed. I work in the slaughterhouse, me. Back there. He pointed briefly down and across the road.

Two young girls – teenagers, dressed in pastel shorts and vests – stepped out onto the road just where he was pointing. They looked at him and giggled, whispering something. A small white terrier was nosing around their legs, but they were oblivious to it. They trotted across to the three men, the dog following, then hurried on past and waited behind them, leaning whispering against the wall of the hotel the big man had come from. The loud, heavy stranger tracked them with his eyes, then stared off into space, finally turning back to the slaughterhouse worker.

Is it still the old gun you use there, then?

The slaughterman blinked. Well, aye, for the cows, like, with the bolt, aye. But you've got your prongs mind, for the lambs.

The big man laid the rod back against the bus-stop and lifted two fingers to either side of his head, just behind the ears. Like that, he said. Right pal?

Aye! The slaughterman brightened, gratified that the stranger knew something about his work. He grinned conspiratorially. Hey, I tell you what though, new buckets came in the day and the first thing I had to say to the boss was naw, no good, send them back! Send them back? he says. Aye, I say. Too big! I say. Aye, they were too big for the little plastic chutes, too big to go under them like. He shook his head, still grinning, then took another drag on his cigarette.

There was quiet for a while.

That's my place there, the big man said, thumbing back at the hotel where the girls still leaned, whispering. Chef. Head Chef. He glared at them as if expecting some kind of challenge.

They both nodded.

Tell you what pal, it's you we get our steaks from I reckon, he said to the slaughterman.

Well, I wouldn't know that like, but aye, mebbe.

Aye. You kill the bastards all wrong, mind.

The slaughterman looked up at him, blinking again.

Right enough you do, pal. That bolt thing, it's a bastard for bruising. Ruins the off-cuts every shot, and your good cuts too, now and again. The bruising spreads, ken? Toughens the meat. Toughens it all to fuck.

The fisherman watched the chef's face, wondering. It sounded like bullshit, but there wasn't any sign. The slaughterman twisted his face doubtfully.

Listen pal, said the chef, what colour is a lobster when you catch it, eh?

It's…eh, it's orange, like.

No, no pal, when it's fucking *caught,* ken? *Alive.*

The slaughterman fidgeted with his cigarette. Aye, well brown like.

No, no it's fucking *blue,* eh? It goes red because the hot water you drop it into touches its brain, and that makes it bruise, pal. It's a big fucking *bruise,* all that pink and red. He turned to the fisherman. Ken? he said. A *bruise.* Whoosh. All over. Now see what I mean about the bolt and your cow and that, eh? It's all in the fucking *brain,* pal. He tapped his skull and leered.

Aye, mebbe like. He shrugged and went back to his cigarette.

The dog that had crossed the road behind the girls suddenly appeared at the slaughterman's feet, sniffing around his legs and speckled boots. For a while it got distracted by the empty ice-cream tub, but soon went back to the boots. The slaughterman watched the dog for a while, then caught the fisherman's eye.

It's all that offal he's smelling, eh? On the boots like. He grinned happily.

They both looked back down at the dog. It started to lick at one of the ankles. Then it took hold of a lace with small sharp teeth and the slaughterman nudged it away with a yellow steel toecap. It tried again and got another, sharper dig in the ribs. It gave up and lay down in the sun near the boots, panting but still staring at the toecaps.

The fisherman saw the girl from the cafe come out carrying a long wooden pole. She used it to push back the awning over the window, went back inside with it and reappeared moments later with a stooping man who locked the door behind them. They both got into his car which pulled off sharply, u-turned across the road and accelerated up the street past the bus-stop. She looked straight ahead as they sped by.

The two younger girls suddenly appeared at his side, brushing between him and the chef. They made a show of looking up and down the empty road, then rushed across, the leading girl snorting with stifled laughter. Both men watched them trot over into the garage forecourt and on into its refreshments shop.

Those two crazy bitches came in on the bus with me this morning, the chef said in a low voice. Giggling and whispering like that all the fucking way. Aye by Christ. He turned to the slaughterman, pushing with his tongue behind both lips before speaking. Anyway pal, I don't go much for steak anyway, he said.

Eh, I love a bit of steak, me, the slaughterman replied, interested again. It's great, steak is.

Nah. You ken what I like? I like to get a wee bit garlic, right? Tomatoes, chopped onions, those fucking courgettes, aye? And a few mushrooms, and cover the lot with fucking brandy, after you've made a ring of sliced potatoes first mind, – fried nice, ken? – and covered in cheese, plenty of herbs like, and set fire to the fucking brandy and serve it up like that, with all the fucking flames still going. Right fucking tasty, that is. He was swaying as he spoke.

Aye, said the slaughterman, bewildered.

Bugger to eat mind, said the fisherman.

The chef worked the underside of his lips again before answering. Aye, all those flames, he said sourly. That's right.

The street was busier now, traffic getting back from the city, the fisherman guessed. The heavy air was starting to taste of dust and petrol. The chef had taken hold of the rod and was fingering it through the cloth again. The fisherman watched him, then looked over to the slaughterman.

He was staring away across the wide street and the fisherman couldn't tell if he was grinning or wincing into the low sun. The dog at his feet was alert now, flicking his head after traffic, sniffing the air. Out of the corner of his eye the fisherman saw the two girls standing at the edge of the garage forecourt, waiting arm in arm for a break in the traffic. He turned to watch them and they teetered forward off the kerb and onto the road. He felt the chef at his side and realised he was tilting the rod in the girls' direction, pointing them out. I tell you what, son, he said in a suddenly low, restful voice, if I was your age I'd have those two up in those hills alright, the pair of them, up in the bushes up there. That's what they want when they're that age by Christ, up in the bushes like that, they can't help it, I'm telling you, straight up son, straight fucking up.

The young fisherman looked along the angle of the rod to the girls, still hesitating, just beyond the kerb; then up to the hills in the distance at their backs. There were no bushes, only the bare folds of the slopes, and out beyond the slopes a smoky, hot haze, up above them an empty evening sky, and somewhere amongst them a cold, quick river.

# UNDERWORLD

This morning at work I found an overnight email from Angus Grant, a name I hadn't given a thought to for more than twenty years. The message was brief. He'd seen in the funeral notices of the local newspaper that Jessie Frayn had been cremated earlier that week. Seeing her name like that, he wrote, had brought back a few memories, and made him curious, and he'd taken it into his head to search me out. Was I who he thought I was? he was wondering.

I deleted it without replying, hoping that would be an end to it.

My chambers at Gray's Inn Court are at basement level and whenever I feel, as any barrister sometimes must, tired of the awful comedy of the work, I push away my case files, light a single illicit indoor cigarette and watch the brisk black shoes and legs of colleagues, judges and secretaries, all the automata of the law, scissoring back and forth above my window. I lower the heavy sash to let out the smoke and listen to snatches of conversation, the clicking of heels, or in city drizzle the *swip* of a briefcase over the skirts of a waxed raincoat. A vague feeling of reckoning comes to me in the language of all those anonymous sounds, and it reassures and calms me.

This morning I smoked a second cigarette, slowly, and then a third before heaving the window shut. By mid-morning I was home again, here at my window desk, the cold room at my back somehow strange to me at this hour of a working day. Before starting to write I sit still for a while, looking east over Earl's Court and beyond to the overcast heart of the city. It's October already, and when I try to recall the early summer months of recriminations, fighting and separation nothing comes except a vague impression of long, stifling nights of heat. Suddenly, I feel an almost overwhelming desire to sleep, but it's not tiredness, I know, so I resist it, and begin.

To fill the months between finishing my school exams and studying Law in London I took a summer job at Driscoll's, a general store and newsagent's opposite the sea wall in the village. My parents had moved to the Scottish coast near the Holy Loch from Portsmouth in my early teens. My father, a naval engineer, worked on the nuclear submarines, and I suppose my own life too soon took on something of a stealthy, trespassing quality. I was the oldest in my year and found it easy to satisfy myself with a certain type of disaffected local girl – the clever rebels, bored and contemptuous of the less worldly-wise village boys – but in the main I was a silent, foreign intruder at the High School, made few acquaintances and wanted even fewer, and was glad to escape my days there for the menial work of a summer job.

I was interviewed in the back room of Driscoll's by the petite, blonde, forty-something manager, Mrs Campbell. I can picture her now, removing and folding her gold-rimmed glasses before starting the interview. She read the questions from a clipboard and ticked boxes as she went. And do you smoke? she finished up by asking.

No, I lied.

Good. She ticked a final box and looked me up and down, lips pursing. Well, you seem clean and smart and strong enough to do any lifting. Start at seven tomorrow – that gives an hour for training.

Seven, I confirmed, and made instinctively to shake her hand, confusing her.

At first I was allowed only to re-fill the shelves, label stock and clean the floors. The shop had three long narrow aisles, a till near the exit and a video rental section at the back so it wasn't difficult to find ways of making myself look busy when Mrs Campbell was watching out for me. If she was safely out of sight in her office, I smoked at the back door or loafed around in the quiet aisles with the part-time assistant, a badly acned, gangly seventeen year old who spun long, improbable stories about his ready supplies of hard drugs and his links with the local criminal underworld. That was Angus Grant. When Angus wasn't around, I flirted with the girl on the till, Jessie Frayn. Hardly a day went by without me offering to polish the plastic name tag pinned over her small left breast or snapping my duster at the highland cow she kept as a mascot on the till-side counter.

Jessie was a pretty, lively-faced brunette of sixteen, and a dwarf. She stood no taller than three-four or five, I would guess. Sharp-witted and cheery, she gave me plenty of encouragement to tease her. The real attraction, though, was her self-possession, the deep reserve I quickly sensed in her, hard and hidden under all the tolerance and self-deprecating laughter. I wouldn't have put it into words at that time, but there was a correspondence, it seemed to me, between the compactness of her body and her stubborn defences. Sometimes, when I pushed the teasing too far, I caught a glimpse of a more vulnerable core, but only a glimpse, and I could never be sure. The congruence made her seem somehow complete and self-sufficient, armoured against me in a way I'd never encountered in a girl before. When I left the shop each evening she slipped from my mind as clean as water through a net, but while she was physically present, a captive audience, perched on the cushions of her check-out chair, I circled and probed at her, body and mind, rearranging her moods as if she was a puzzle of blocks laid out to test me.

As the weeks went on, I found myself more and more often joining Jessie in the back room where she was allowed to spend ten minute coffee and toilet breaks on quiet afternoons, Mrs Campbell minding the till. The room was stuffy and windowless, over-furnished with a three-drawered, forest-green filing cabinet, a dark wooden desk where Mrs Campbell spread her paperwork, and a couple of lapsed armchairs. Two taps and a tiny sink with a draining board backed onto the staff toilet next door. When the flush was pulled, the taps in the back room gurgled. I liked the claustrophobic intimacy of the place. Jessie would sit in one of the broken-down armchairs, her feet barely brushing the worn carpet; I'd perch myself on the edge of Mrs Campbell's desk and entertain her, sometimes passing on one of Angus's gangland fantasies, sometimes recommending films or literature to her, neither of which she knew much about. Always towards the end of these performances I found myself nestling my coffee mug over an almost painful erection.

At the end of the fourth week Mrs Campbell told me I could get a small raise if I helped with the accounts and stock-taking. Later, as if to reward my willingness to take on the extra responsibility, she poured me a coffee in the back room. Tell me a bit about yourself, she said. You're leaving after the summer, aren't you?

In early August Jessie took a week off sick. Without her to tease I spent more time helping Mrs Campbell with the accounts while Angus kept the till. Late one afternoon in the back room she confided how and why her marriage was failing.

I shouldn't be talking like this, she admitted, but you're the only sensitive person I see nowadays. You're a thinker. A *feeler*. I've had enough of the other kind, she whispered fiercely. Enough! She took a deep breath and sighed it out. It's your age. You're unspoilt, she said, suddenly flat and matter of fact again.

On the Friday after closing, she led me into the stock room.

Afterwards, she seemed disappointed. She was brisk in the way she snapped her pants and tights back over her hips and seemed almost angry as she smoothed her black skirt flat over the fronts of her thighs. But then, I remember thinking, she'd been brisk in rucking the skirt up in the first place.

Was that alright? I asked. In the dark grotto of the stock room my voice sounded foreign to myself, and I remember wishing I hadn't spoken.

Yes. She smoothed her hair, avoiding eye contact. Silly boy, she said.

The next Monday Jessie was at her till again. On my coffee break with her that morning I found myself almost shy with the pleasure of having her back. Jessie too seemed galvanised. She waited for me at the door of the back room while I used the toilet, then nudged me as I squeezed past her. Her shoulder slipped from my hip and tilted into my groin, resting briefly on the hardness already there. Make us coffee, she said, as open-faced and happy as I could ever remember seeing her. You've got to spoil me – it's my birthday tomorrow, she announced, following me in and falling back into her seat. She raised her arms as if to celebrate, and I noticed with a strange feeling of pleasure that they hardly cleared the low back of the chair.

Is that why you're buzzing?

Why else? she said, blushing.

Later, I smoked at the back door with Angus. Just behind the shop a tiny burn trickled along a pebbled ditch and in fine weather we'd escape to its bank for as long as we could get away with, kicking pebbles into the water and finally flicking our cigarette butts into the clear stream. A concrete culvert, its round mouth a yard or so in diameter, took the burn under the buildings to an outlet on the sea wall. Whenever Angus was scolded by Mrs Campbell, which was often, he would hawk and spit out his frustration into the water between streams of smoke. I could have this place burned down, man, he would tell me. Burned to the fucking *ground*. I just need to give the word, ken? On calmer days he'd tell me that a fat albino rat had its nest a little way inside the culvert, though of course I never saw it. Moby Dick, he called her. A big white bitch rat, man, he'd insist, leading its fucking babies. He'd shake his head, ruefully.

I saw you leave with the boss the other night, Angus muttered, now. She patted yer arse when you walked off, man.

I laughed and tossed the last of my cigarette into the ditch.

He sighed. I tell you so many things, man. Things that risk my fucking *life*, ken? And all you do is play high and fucking mighty with me. He shook his head, disappointed, the way my father might have. I mean, fuck's sake, just tell me how you did it, he said.

For Jessie's birthday I lifted some vodka miniatures and a bottle of cola on my way to the back room. She was waiting for me but her good mood of the day before had passed. She sat behind the desk on Mrs Campbell's revolving chair and stared accusingly at me.

Of course, I thought: Angus had told her. I fixed the vodkas and we drank quickly, the conversation stilted.

You know what Angus asked me yesterday? she said, using her hands on the desk to swivel the chair first one way then the other.

No. What? I said, bracing myself.

He wanted to know what was the right name for people like me – midgets or dwarves.

I started to laugh, then realised she wasn't joining in and stopped. What did you say?

I said what you call things doesn't make them what they are.

I think I did laugh, then. Aye it does, ken, I said, mimicking Angus.

She levelled a sudden hard stare at me. Well. At least he wouldn't say it the way you would, she said, and I knew with a strange sense of revelation that underneath the teasing and desire we were enemies, really, and I wanted her small secret body more than ever.

She looked away, silent for a while. Our life expectancy's normal, she said abruptly, slurring a little after the vodka.

Oh, I said, confused.

People think it isn't, she said, and grimaced. I don't feel very well. Shouldn't drink on an empty stomach. Help me off this stupid chair, she said. I hate falling.

I finished my drink and took hold of her under the arms. It was the first time I'd touched her properly, feeling the firmness of the flesh under her shop blouse, and when I lifted her I was surprised at the weight. I'd expected her to be no heavier than a child but there was an adult density to her frame that caught me unawares and for a moment nearly unbalanced me. Turning, I lifted her higher, with some effort, and set her down on top of the filing cabinet.

Whee, she said coldly, you know how to show a girl a good time.

I stood still, indecisive, the flat soles of her shoes butting against my chest. I wondered if she could feel the knock of my heart through the soles. The thought stirred up something morbid in me and I swayed back from the contact.

I feel dizzy, she said, closing her eyes, and I glanced down at her legs sheathed in black nylon, projecting over the edge of the cabinet. On an impulse I took hold of her ankles, cupping them on the undersides, just touching the first bulge of the calf muscles beyond them. When she said nothing I slid my palms onto the roundness of her legs, struck by the solid, compacted strength there.

She opened her eyes and leaned forward to take hold of my forearms. Are you fooling with Mrs Campbell? She jerked the words out, as if short of breath.

No, I said. Why?

Because if you are, you shouldn't be playing around like this. Her fingers tightened on my arms.

Like what? I said, forcing my palms along her short calves to the backs of her knees. Trapped in her narrow work skirt her legs could hardly open more than a few inches, though for a moment I felt her strain to part them wider. I tugged her towards me.

No. Lift me down now, she said.

That evening, before leading me into the stock room, Mrs Campbell told me she had decided to let Jessie go.

What for? I blurted guiltily, remembering the vodka.

She shrugged. Angus is fine on the till now, and I know it's terrible of me but I can't stand to look at her day in and day out. She sighed. Angus is very slow, but he's coming along, isn't he?

A little later, for the first time in our affair, Mrs Campbell undressed for me. She brought a blanket in from her car and laid it on the stock room's concrete floor, then straddled and milked me so expertly I came with noisy, helpless, gasping sobs that she tried to muffle with her palm.

That was amazing, I whispered afterwards, stretched out alongside her, breathless in the warm gloom.

Good, she said and sat up, feeling around her feet for her clothes.

A month passed after Jessie was laid off, and then in my last week before leaving for London she called me. I was in my bedroom, already choosing and packing, surrounded by books, record albums and folders.

I was wondering if I could borrow some books. The ones you used to tell me I should read, she said. She paused, then added defensively: I can post them back to you, if you let me know where you are.

Of course, I said.

I could cook for you, she said, before you go. Friday, if you want.

I'd like that, I told her.

When Friday closing came I told Mrs Campbell I had to visit a relative in hospital and couldn't stay late.

I didn't ask you to, she snapped, and I knew I'd lied poorly.

Jessie's flat was in a quiet corner of the town's housing scheme, a cul-de-sac that I remembered using for reversing and parking practice when learning to drive two years before. It was the first time I'd been anywhere near there since, and now, in the mellow, late summer light I felt faintly nostalgic at rediscovering it.

She answered the door almost at once and I followed her into a small, brightly lit kitchen off the hall.

A casserole of some sort was simmering on the electric hob. To reach it, Jessie climbed a red plastic step, the kind you see in the children's sections of libraries. She stirred busily, avoiding eye contact.

Do you share? I asked.

Uh huh. My sister. She turned to me finally, got down off the step and slid it with her foot to a set of cupboards. That's why everything's at your height. If it was my place I'd have things more convenient.

As she spoke I realised that I was obscurely disappointed by the familiar scale, the ordinariness of the things around me. What had I hoped for? I wondered.

Don't watch me cook, she said. Can you pour me some wine?

Do you want to see the books? I said.

She nodded. Later though. Go through and watch TV if you like – I'll bring the food when it's ready.

All along the hall and in the living room small, dark oil paintings hung against the pale walls. They were completely abstract: either planes of thick, gloomy colour – greys, browns and greens, mainly – or more or less geometric shapes against lowering backgrounds. They were very ugly.

Where did you get the paintings? I asked when she brought more wine for me.

She laughed. I painted them, she said. Do you like them?

I don't know. I don't think I understand them.

You're not supposed to. Most people who see them hate them. She moved to peer more closely at the nearest. I like it when they annoy people. That's why I paint them, I think – to irritate people. I don't know. I haven't painted one for months now. She shrugged. Since I met you, she added suddenly, her voice dipping. She went back to the kitchen.

After eating we sat and drank while Jessie asked me about the books. Were any of them poetry? she wanted to know.

No, I said, surprised. I didn't know you wanted poetry.

Not *just* poetry. But maybe one of them could have been poetry.

Sorry, no poetry, I said. The curtains in the room were wide open and by that time the late summer dusk was already turning into night.

You've read all of these? she asked.

I nodded.

She picked up one of the paperbacks and stared hard at the cover. It makes me feel stupid, she announced.

What does?

That you've read so much more than me.

What time does your sister come in? I asked.

She's away tonight; on a training course. Jessie leaned forward and poured herself another full glass, draining the last of our third or fourth bottle of wine. You're going away soon, aren't you?

I nodded.

To be a lawyer.

That's right. I remember the ambivalence in her tone, and still can't judge if it was mocking or envious. It stung me, anyway, even through the drink, and I fell quiet.

She drank a little more then pushed herself off the couch and went through into the hall. I sat brooding for a time, then got up and made my way to the bathroom, weaving through the dark.

There was a step in front of the toilet, a white plastic moulding, and another at the foot of the washbasin. After using the toilet and rinsing my hands, I examined myself in the mirror. My face felt clumsy and numb. When I tried out different winning expressions I seemed to keep repeating the same half comical, half sinister leer.

Back in the hall, Jessie called to me from one of the rooms opposite the kitchen. The door opened onto her bedroom and she was in bed, sitting up pale in the dark, the sheets pulled high to cover her breasts.

Come in. If you want, she said.

I nodded.

She watched intently as I undressed, staring through the gloom with open curiosity. As soon as I sat next to her, naked, she slid down the bed and took hold of my erection with both cool hands, bringing a yelp from me that made her giggle. Are you a virgin? she asked, once we'd both settled.

No, I laughed.

She pressed closer, opening her legs over the long muscle of my thigh. I don't mind. It's better if you know what you're doing. She began moving her hands, slowly and still in tandem.

When she said she was ready, I rolled on top and reached down to guide myself.

Hurting? I asked, seeing her wince.

Yes.

I hesitated.

No. Go on, she gasped.

Her eyes were tight shut now, and free from her stare I remember studying her face. It was unpleasantly white, and closed like a fist. I remember thinking of the early days of summer and wondering at all the times I'd puzzled over her privacies. They were clear to me now; plain and simple after all. With a grunt I was through, Jessie shrieking as she broke, then moaning with a strange, distant sound as I fell into my rhythm.

I left after midnight. At the edge of the scheme I crossed the High Street and made for the sea-front though it wasn't the quickest way home. An early autumnal westerly had picked up off the Atlantic and it buffeted me as I walked. Striding into it I let my arms fall loose at my sides, waiting for the feeling of lift as each gust urged them outwards. I felt weirdly pure: weightless and cleansed of all confusions, all complications. I was leaving, leaving, leaving. I could have flown into the air, a scrap of paper in the wind. There was no depth to life, I remember thinking suddenly, and it seemed like a moment of final clarity and truth to me, the great lesson of my long, trivial summer. There was a shifting, fascinating surface to people and the things they felt and said, but underneath it all was just a stony simplicity. Life was like the burn behind the shop, I thought as I leaned into the wind, drunk and grimly happy; a little stream no deeper than its skin; mirrors over a pebble bed.

I didn't notice Angus until I heard my name called from the promenade bus shelter.

Where you heading, man? Angus was hunched in a dark, heavy trench coat. A wedge of greasy hair blew across his face and he scooped it back theatrically.

I gestured vaguely, stepping into the shelter.

He held out a small flask of spirits.

I shook my head and Angus shrugged before taking a nip from it.

So. When is it ye're off now? He turned away to hawk and spit.

Sunday.

Angus nodded. Law, he said portentously.

I looked away across the street. The steel shutters were down over the windows of the shop and with each gust of wind they rattled faintly.

You'll be one o' the enemy, man. Enemy o' the underworld, ken? The wind dislodged a clump of hair again and this time Angus let it hang there a while, shielding him, before dragging it back.

I laughed, turning to face him.

There was something new in his voice, I remember, an air of superiority, or contempt now that he was out of his shop apron and had the night at his back.

It didn't matter. I was leaving soon, for good, and the thought filled me again with a sudden surge of immense satisfaction. I stared past Angus and out over the sea wall. Black waves streaked with foam were rolling in fast out of the night. One after another they boomed dully into the sea wall and shattered with a boiling hiss. I remember imagining the great chains of the northern currents, deep and cold, stretching all the vast way to Greenland, Newfoundland, America. We stared out at the waves together a while and then without a word or sign to Angus I left him and crossed the empty road, hurrying.

For a long time after, or at least for what seemed like a long time then, in my twenties, I kept the occasional letters that Jessie sent, though I never responded. In all fairness, they never invited reply. Like her dark, cramped paintings they were only masks. Their meaning was in their effect and even at their most fevered – and some were startlingly erotic – they were always impersonal, always opaque.

Eventually, on a bored whim, some fifteen years ago, maybe more, I carried them all in to work and fed them to the office shredder. I changed addresses often in those days and no new letters ever found me to replace them.

It often seems to me that there's something principled in the most hardened of my clients – those who can never confess, even to themselves. True criminals are the best of Idealists: they remember only on their own terms, and know that the whole world changes with each gratification. And why shouldn't they come to think that way? Criminals are the courts' apprentices.

Outside my window the late afternoon sky is blank, not promising brightness or rain. When I stand I can see the commuters, a dark quiet river, flowing homewards along the street below. Behind them, more travellers, an endless stream, spill out of Earl's Court underground, almost all of them as they emerge glancing up at the colourless, unreadable sky, frowning an instant as if confused, or wary. How many thousands of times have I done the same thing myself? All trespassers. All following one another until they vanish, one by one, into cars and buses and buildings on the way to being alone again.

# FIVE NIGHT STAY

Hamilton picked her out easily despite the August festival crowds swirling about the station concourse. Something about her – maybe her stillness in so much swarming movement, or her awkward, gangly tallness, striking in a girl so young – seemed to deflect like a magic circle the bustle and press all around her.

He was already late but paused anyway on the narrow iron walkway overlooking the crowds. She was staring towards the Waverley café and bar. Now that she was here, finally, he was hesitant. At the thought of greeting her, of having to find the right words, a heavy reluctance, like drowsiness, seemed to soak through his brain and limbs. If he could slip away now, without consequences, he would turn back, he confessed to himself. She was so tall and awkward and alone, there with her mother's bulging white suitcase at her feet.

But he had fought her mother for exactly this: a longer time with his own daughter, and there was no backing out now. Whatever you think of me, I've got a natural right, he'd insisted the last time they quarrelled, a father's *right* to get to know his kid. Look at her, he'd hissed, gesturing towards his car where she was sitting, out of earshot but watching them through the glass; *look* at her, for Christ's sakes. She won't *be* a kid much longer the way she's going.

It was only a month since he'd made that last trip south to Leatherhead, but now, watching her unseen from above, he suddenly felt as if years had passed and he realised he was gripping hard on the walkway rail, his hands slippery with sweat. She was still facing the café, her long, bare arms hanging limp at her sides. He freed his fingers and made his way down to her. As his feet clanked on the walkway's iron steps he looked up at the high, dirty glass panes roofing the platforms, and through them to the tops of buildings at street level where the hot, dusty city thundered and roared. Marian, let's get out of here, he almost shouted when he reached her from behind, and she jumped a little, startled.

In the taxi she handed him a letter out of the front pocket of her suitcase.

From your mother? he asked, and she nodded, reticent as always. He opened the unmarked envelope. The list inside seemed to have been scrawled in a hurry. One instruction was blotted out very thoroughly, and only his daughter's gaze stopped him holding the paper up to the light from the cab window.

Arrange horses. No horses=ponies

History/castles etc=fine. Scottish history=upsetting?
<u>No</u> swimming.
Growing pains at night=normal. Bone cancer=what she thinks.
Periods=heavy. Plenty <u>red</u> <u>meat</u>.
No conversations God – angels – death – afterlife etc.
If raining=shopping? Sometimes=upsetting.

He folded the sheet into an inside jacket pocket. The taxi had been crawling through traffic and now it stopped dead behind a line of open-topped buses. So, he said, meeting her stare, how about this weather?

As if in answer, she turned to gaze out at the sweltering tourists and shoppers jostling alongside the cab. I expected Scotland might be a bit cooler, she admitted, and plucked the cotton of her fitted vest away from her flat, damp chest.

It will be in the highlands, he said, and she nodded, frowning faintly at someone or something in the crowd. We'll be high up, he added, then cleared his throat and waited for the cab to lurch forward again.

That evening he ordered pizza to the flat and presented Marian with a heavy, oatmeal coloured, cavalry twill riding jacket as a thirteenth birthday present. That's why you only got a card last week, he said. I wanted to give you your real present myself.

Oh, she said, thank you. She held it up in front of her for a moment, then worked her arms into the stiff sleeves.

Surprise, he said, and she smiled.

The jacket was short in the arms but fitted well enough on the body, he thought. She lifted her arms out from her sides then lowered them again.

It's really good material. Very expensive. The best. That's why it's a wee bit stiff to get into. But that's good if you ever take a fall.

She nodded agreement.

The sleeves can be let out. I checked that, he added. I told them it might need that. It's bespoke, he said.

She nodded again, seeming pleased with it, Hamilton judged, in her own undemonstrative way. She thanked him a second time, hugged him woodenly, then removed and set the jacket back on its varnished hanger before sitting down to eat.

Hamilton waited a while, then glanced up at her. You want to take it with us to the hotel? I've booked some pony-trekking for you.

She blinked and stopped chewing, then shook her head.

No? Why not?

Colouring, she stared hard at the slice of pizza in her fingers. It's not the kind of thing they'd wear, she said at last. The pony-trekking crowd.

Oh, he said, and laughed as she gave a pained smile back. Okay. I didn't think of that.

She shifted in her seat.

You'll wear it once you're back home, though? For your serious riding? Of course.

That's fine then, he said, and watched her finish her food.

* * *

They left mid-morning for the drive north. Without telling Hamilton why, Marian took a brief but intense interest in Fettes School as they passed by. Then she settled back, eyes closed, sealed off from him by the ear buds of her iPod.

The weather held fine through Perthshire but by noon a grey, level bank of clouds seemed to wait on the northern horizon for them, barely moving but shielding more and more of the blue sky as the road climbed from bright birch woods to the snow gates before Drumochter. Just after two, Hamilton found the small hotel, tucked at the back of its village. A light rain was drifting in the air, speckling the windscreen. The clouds he had been driving towards plated the sky completely now. Marian was sleeping, and he was hungry and stiff and irrationally vexed that she wasn't awake to share his discomfort. He stopped the engine, got out onto the pebbled parking space at the end of the drive and left the car door ajar while he went in to the Reception.

The proprietor, a small, neat, energetic-seeming woman, was busy with paperwork behind the desk. Her hair was completely grey but her face was smooth and almost youthful. She took a moment to sign something, then smiled up at him. Mr Hamilton, she said decisively.

That's right.

It's just you and a coach party of Japanese arriving today, she said, as if to explain her certainty. Maybe one more late tonight, but only if they make it cross-country, she added doubtfully. She spoke with a firm Yorkshire accent. It sounded much stronger in person than it had over the phone, Hamilton thought. She seemed to study his face for a moment, then looked out of a side window onto the drive. With a tiny, brisk dip of the head she acknowledged his solitary parked car, dark and heavy on the shingle drive. You're with your daughter, it says in my book. Just you and your daughter?

Just the two of us.

Well, she said, and passed him a form to sign. I'll take you to your rooms myself. The girls are off for the afternoon. She turned to take two keys from brass hooks on the wall behind her, and Hamilton looked around him and peered up the broad hall towards the shadowy staircase as if noting the girls' absence, whoever they were.

Their rooms were part of a long, low converted stable running at right angles to the main building. At their back was a small courtyard unbounded on its other two sides. A dead fountain, crusted with lichen, was its only feature and just beyond the yard's boundary, where the cobbles gave onto a rough, uncultivated field, stood three small caravans. They were axle-deep in grass and thistles but obviously inhabited: a full washing line was strung up close by them and a shadow of movement flickered behind one of the windows. The rain had cleared from the air now and a cool breeze had sprung up. The blouses and underclothes on the line swung out in the gusts.

Here we are, the manager said, and Hamilton halted behind her while she unlocked a door and led them both inside. Your own door is the next one along, she said, turning to Marian and handing her a key, but we can go through to it from here – the rooms are connected. She moved to the narrow connecting door and opened it to show them. It bolts from both sides, she said and slid a small bolt back and forth. There's a mini-bar in this room but not in yours, I'm afraid, she said to Marian again, smiling briefly. She went through to the adjoining room and Marian followed after her with her case. Hamilton yawned and sat heavily on the nearest of his twin beds. Through the net skirt covering the glass panel in his door he could make out the white of the caravans. The room's main window was in the opposite wall, looking out onto the drive. It was small and set deep into the bulky, crude stone blocks of the old building. From where Hamilton sat on the bed all that could be seen through it was the solid grey of the sky. He stretched forward and with the tips of his fingers eased open the door of the mini-bar.

We count them up at the end of your stay and add what you've used to the bill, the manager said, surprising him. They were both back through in his room now, behind him. If you need it re-stocked just let me know.

Right, he said, faintly embarrassed. He flicked it shut.

I'll leave you to settle in, then. Unless there's anything else?

Are you hungry? Hamilton asked Marian.

She shook her head.

No? he said, disbelieving.

Chef's not coming up from the village until four, the manager broke in, but I can get you crisps or peanuts from the bar. Or you could try one of the cafés on the High Street.

We'll maybe do that, he said, concealing his irritation. A walk's probably what we need after that drive.

I'm fine, Marian said. I'll just stay here.

The manager looked from Hamilton to Marian, then back at Hamilton again. Well, let me know if you need me, she said, and beamed at them before leaving.

Only one café was open in the village and the best Hamilton could get in the way of hot food was a rubbery bacon roll. He bolted it, swilling down the last stale mouthful with the dregs of his coffee, then hurried back up the road to the hotel. A vague feeling of unease had followed him ever since he had left his room and he felt oppressed by the thick clouds cloaking the village. The last of the climb was steep and his skin felt clammy under his clothes when he arrived finally at his door. He glanced across the courtyard while he fumbled for his keys. There seemed to be no movement in the caravans opposite now, and no light in any of their windows. The washing on their line hung perfectly still though the smell of damp grass seemed to carry somehow from the overgrown field to him, filling his nostrils. Quietly, he let himself in.

Marian was sleeping, curled tightly under the coverlet. Hamilton had half-expected the connecting door to be bolted, and when it had opened, its bottom edge sighing over the carpet and giving onto the private gloom of her curtained room, he felt strangely moved and comforted. For a while he watched her, then went through to his own bed and set his alarm to wake him for dinner.

They were handed menus by a young girl, scarred from a harelip, who intercepted them as they made their way down the hall in search of the dining area. She wore a simple uniform – white blouse and straight black skirt – and spoke broken English with an eastern European accent. Please, she said, smiling shyly, and directed them into a conservatory sitting area which gave onto the dining room proper. Would you like to drink? While you choose? she asked, still smiling, once they had taken the menus from her and settled on the wicker couch.

What would you like? Hamilton asked Marian.

Just water, please.

Just water? You sure?

Just water, she repeated. Please.

A bottle of water? the waitress asked.

Just tap water, Marian said. She was blushing now.

The waitress seemed confused. She looked at Hamilton.

Just a glass – from the tap, Hamilton said, making a turning motion with his hand.

Ah, she said, and laughed a little. Yes, she said.

Gin and tonic for me, he added.

Yes, she said. Gin and tonic. She left, smiling.

Hamilton watched her go. Her dark, glossy hair was tied severely in a bun but let loose would fall down thick and ringletted, he decided. She walked with a quick, light motion, on delicate legs, almost skipping through to the bar.

She's pretty, Marian said, then leaned forward and picked up a stuffed photograph album from the coffee table in front of them. Hamilton sat back and surveyed the garden outside the conservatory. A long, closely mown lawn, broken only by a court of croquet hoops, stretched to a far wall, low and tumbledown. Beyond that was a field of rape, dull gold under the heavy evening clouds. Dark firs, cypresses and a few Scots pines bordered the entire length of the lawn. A single rabbit, feeding at the edge of a nearby flower border, lifted its head and paused, suddenly wary. Look at the rabbit, he said to Marian, but she was absorbed in the album.

The door to the bar swung open and the waitress approached with a tray. She bent gracefully to settle it on the low coffee table, then handed them their glasses. Were they ready to order? she wanted to know.

We'll relax a little while here first, if that's alright, Hamilton said.

Oh, of course, she said, eagerly.

It's very peaceful, isn't it? And a lovely view. He smiled, meeting her eyes, until she turned away and gathered up the tray.

Marian waited for her to leave and then fished with her fingertips for the slice of lime in her water. Pinching the rind, she shook off most of the wet and then leaned forward for the heavy brass ashtray on the table.

If you don't want that, drop it in mine, honey, Hamilton intervened. He held out his glass and she plopped it in. He swirled the gin, making the ice faintly chime, and winked at her. What's in the album?

The family, I think. I recognise the woman, but she's got a husband and two boys in the photos. It shows how they changed the building into a hotel.

That's interesting, said Hamilton. The rabbit was feeding again, head bowed, and others had appeared in the open too, now. They crouched, dotted about the lawn, static, as if distilled out of the grey atmosphere. There was something unpleasant about them, about their being there so suddenly, unmoving on the big, evening lawn. He could hardly take his eyes off them, though he knew Marian was watching him, wanting his attention.

What's a manse?

A manse? he said, and forced himself to turn from the garden. It's a house for ministers. Church ministers.

This used to be a manse. It says on the front page of the menu.

He opened his own menu and read the brief history of the building. Well, what would you like to eat? he said after finishing, turning the page. She was still staring at the story of the building.

Chicken, if it's there, she murmured.

You don't want steak? They do great steak. It's Aberdeen Angus. Or lamb?

She shuddered. No lamb, she said. Just chicken.

Okay, he said. It's got garlic in it – that alright?

She nodded, still reading.

A different waitress, a plump, limp-haired blonde with a Scottish accent, took their order and led them to their table. To Hamilton's relief, Marian ate well and quickly though between each course she slipped away to wash her hands and was gone for several minutes at a time. At the table, whenever either of the waitresses came in to the room she followed their movements with obvious fascination.

The manager herself came to the table with the desserts menu. How have the girls been? she wanted to know. The blond girl's from the village, she said. That's Helen. But Beata's Slovakian. She's the darker girl. We're getting more and more of them over for summer jobs now. They work hard, she went on, lowering her voice as Beata entered from the bar, carrying a coffee-pot to another table, but I have to train them myself and their English isn't the best. She rolled her eyes.

She's been fine, said Hamilton. Hasn't she, Marian?

Marian nodded.

Slovakia, he said. That's a long way to come for a summer job.

The manager shrugged. It's the way Europe's going, isn't it? Everywhere's the same now. She's here with her twin sister, Marta. They're identical except for the scar. She stroked her upper lip, surreptitiously. Nice girls, she concluded decisively. And the food?

Excellent, Hamilton said.

Good. I'll tell chef.

They live in the caravans? The girls?

That's right, she said, and opened a pad to take down their orders. I'll send one of the girls through for your plates, she finished cheerfully, tapping out a full stop and snapping the notepad shut.

One of the older girls at school has a scar like that, Marian said once the manager was out of earshot.

A harelip?

Is that an insulting name to call it?

No, he said, surprised. He thought for a moment. No, I don't think so. I think it makes you look unusual but not ugly.

No, it's not ugly, is it?

It makes her shy, though. You can tell by the way she smiles.

The girl at school or the waitress?

I meant the waitress. But both of them, in fact, she said.

An elderly Japanese couple appeared in the dining room doorway and half nodded, half bowed in their direction, smiling broadly. They retreated again, silently, and from the direction of the entrance hall Hamilton heard the muffled sounds of voices and fire doors banging shut.

He turned to the window. In the deepening dark only the looming structures of the firs and pines could be made out, all their colour and detail lost. A faint, low mist was lying over the garden and the lawn was empty of life now. The nearer croquet hoops glimmered, just visible in the last of the light.

Can we play croquet tomorrow? she asked, and he realised she was following his gaze.

Why not? he said. If the weather's good.

When the desserts arrived, brought by Beata, Marian again watched the older girl intently until she left the dining room. They ate silently for a while.

Where do you think the rest of the family are? Marian asked suddenly.

Whose family, honey? He glanced up at her.

The woman's family. The ones in the album.

He shook his head. I don't know. They're maybe here and we haven't seen them yet. Maybe the husband does the cooking.

No. She calls him chef.

Well, maybe he does all the odd-jobs around the place, or just does some other job in the village like a bank manager or something while she runs the hotel.

No, she said, with an odd, reluctant finality, and lifted her spoon. Her long, bony hands were red from all the washing.

In bed that night Hamilton opened one of the chilled wines from the mini-bar and read a spy thriller until late, noticing the crack of light under the connecting door only after switching off his bedside lamp and rolling onto his side. Soon, he heard Marian get out of bed to use the bathroom and for some time afterwards she stayed awake, the beam under the door wavering as she moved mysteriously about the room. Finally, he heard the bed creak under her weight again and with a soft click the room went dark. Until sleep came, he thought about the Slovakian girl and the small white caravans in the long grass of the field.

\* \* \*

The next day continued cool and overcast. Just before seven Hamilton watched through the glazed door as one of the twins gathered in the washing from the line, her hair turbaned in a white towel. Soon afterwards she emerged again from the middle caravan and headed for the village on some errand, Hamilton supposed, a small rucksack high on her shoulders. Her rippled hair, hanging long and loose now, was still damp.

After an early breakfast where they were waited on by the manager, he drove Marian a few miles to the outdoor pursuits centre. He had booked her in for two days' pony-trekking, though she could change her mind for either of the days, he insisted to her on the way, if there was anything else she'd rather do. The middle day of their stay he had kept free for them to do something together. How did that sound?

It was fine.

You won't mind a day off from riding?

No, she said, though without much conviction, Hamilton felt.

Back at the hotel his bed had already been made and he felt a brief pang of disappointment. Which of the twins? he wondered, and as he showered and then dried himself he lingered on the thought of them moving quietly about his room. Afterwards, he lay back on the bed, naked and warm-skinned, considering what to do with himself. A gnawing nervous energy had been with him since waking, but he was tempted despite it to spend the day lazily at the hotel; to sit in the conservatory, maybe, and be waited on by the shy, smiling Beata or her sister. Or even to just sit there unattended, hardly noticed, and watch their comings and goings, their pleasant, crisply uniformed routines. Male voices, Japanese, drew closer from the courtyard outside and then passed by his door. Instinctively he covered himself. No, he decided. He would walk into the village and wear out some of his restlessness. Suddenly, he pictured Marian riding, straight-backed and bored on a placid, roly-poly pony, and without warning a feeling of alarm, of panic almost, swept through him. Why? he thought, but could make no sense of it. Frowning, he levered himself from the bed and dressed.

The cramped gift shops on the High Street were depressing to browse, and the thought of the village's main attraction, a folk museum, bored him. He wandered with some curiosity into a narrow, dimly lit game shop and spent some time admiring the mounted salmon flies, the rods and gaffs and the dark, oiled guns in their glass-faced cabinets. At the foot of the High Street he turned into a small, neat memorial park and sat for a while on the stone step of its cenotaph. There were no Hamiltons on the long brass plaque.

A small, clear, quick-running burn partnered the back road past the memorial park and on out of the village. He followed it for half a mile or so, absent-mindedly, until it curved away from the road and was hidden by a thick screen of birches and broom. A little further on, the road climbed steeply to the foothills of the mountains and in the near distance he could see the familiar ruins of an English barracks. Whenever he had driven this far north in years past, or been driven as a boy, he had always noted the barracks, tiny from the main carriageway; remote, it always seemed, from any road or path. It was somehow disappointing for it to be within easy reach now. Slow-moving figures were clambering on the stonework. Turning off from the road he followed a dirt path alongside the burn instead.

Away from the road the land was marshy and tangled. Soon, the bright gravelled bed of the burn widened and gave way to mud and drowned leaves though the water itself remained glass-clear. Then the path took him away from the burn, through a choked copse of alders, and when it met the water again everything had changed: the stream was much deeper and broader, the water was black with peat, and the current seemed to be flowing back on itself, impossibly, towards the village. Bewildered, Hamilton stared down at the black, silent swirls. Then it came to him: somewhere alongside the copse the burn had joined with this stronger, darker stream flowing down from the opposite side of the glen. He smiled at his slow-wittedness and pushed on to where the high bank overlooked a wide, still bend. Maybe a salmon pool, he guessed, though there were no boot prints in the mud round about. Then, looking up, he saw that on the opposite, lower lying bank, a fringe of scrub gave onto a vast, barren expanse of boulders, stones and pebbles. They stretched back almost to the village itself, its rooftops showing tiny and serrated in the grey distance. Apart from a few scattered brambles it seemed as if the entire flood plain had been scraped back to its pale bones; as if, Hamilton thought vaguely, the last of the great glaciers had withered away just a summer or two ago. A thin breeze from the direction of the stone-field rippled the dark pool and he shivered, turning his face from it.

Marian gave little away on the subject of her pony-trek. It had been fine, she assured him on the drive back from the activity centre, and yes, she wanted to go again the day after next, but any further questions were met with polite, non-committal evasions. Are you sure you actually *went* riding? Hamilton jibed at last, because you don't seem to remember very much about it. But she only blushed and he let it go, annoyed with himself for harrying her.

Back at the hotel he was surprised when she called him through to her room almost immediately. Look what the maid did, she said, pointing at her pillow. Two soft toys, a monkey and a dog, had been pushed together on their sides in a comic, stiff-limbed embrace. Marian was delighted. Don't they look cute? she said.

Are they yours? Hamilton asked.

Yes. I just left them on the bedside table, though. She laughed to herself and separated them. I wonder who did it? I think it was Beata.

Why do you think that?

I just do, she said.

They both stared at the toys.

I'll put them back on the table and see if it happens again tomorrow,

Marian announced. She seemed happy now, energised again after the awkward silence of the car. Hamilton knew he should seize the opportunity.

Do you still want to play croquet? he asked.

She thought for a moment. Can I phone mum first?

Of course, honey. He smiled supportively and cleared his throat. You come out when you're ready.

Okay, she said, and waited for him to withdraw.

It took a while for the manager to find the croquet set but eventually she brought it through to the garden for him. He was at the far end, leaning on the ruined wall, looking out over the fields to the lower slopes of the mountains beyond. Their main flanks and peaks were still invisible behind cloud but at least today he could make out their long aprons of scree. The manager called to him from the conservatory doors and made a show of leaving the set on the patio outside them. He waved in reply and she disappeared indoors again.

Marion appeared around the corner of the building as he was still making his way up the length of the lawn. Seeing the set in its battered cardboard box she made straight for it and selected a mallet.

Do you know the rules? she asked when he reached her.

No – you?

It doesn't matter. We can just try to score goals, she said.

Okay, he agreed. How was your mother?

Oh, fine.

Missing you?

She shrugged.

Did you tell her you were having fun?

She nodded.

Come on, he said, and took up two of the wooden balls. Bring me a mallet, honey, he told her, and she followed him to the white hoops of the court.

They started brightly, Marian inventing a series of different challenges and keeping score enthusiastically. But gradually Hamilton found it more and more difficult to concentrate and the constant changes in task seemed disheartening, somehow. It had been a mild early evening when they started, but now a cold easterly was cutting in through the cypresses and the cloud cover was darkening. In the failing light all the foliage around them seemed unnaturally massy and sombre. Marian could sense his boredom, he knew, but he was powerless to throw it off. Eventually he stopped dead, half way to one of the steel hoops, and stared around at the sky. From behind he heard the sharp clack of Marian's mallet and, in the heavy stillness, even the faint buzz of the wooden ball speeding to his heels. It bumped and halted.

I thought you were *playing*, she complained.

He turned, tapping the ball back with his instep.

I thought you *wanted* to play.

Sorry, sweetheart. I'm getting cold, that's all. I should have worn long sleeves.

You should have, she agreed, and regarded him critically. It's no fun if you don't try.

No, I know. He nodded contritely. I'm sorry. Let's go in and get ready for dinner and maybe we can play again tomorrow, if it's warmer.

Before eating, Marian wanted to sit in the conservatory again. She pored over the same unwieldy photograph album while Hamilton sipped his gin, read out choices from the menu to her and tried to engage Beata in snatches of conversation whenever she attended to them. It was difficult and Hamilton wondered if she was exaggerating her poor English.

Ask her about the soft toys, he murmured mischievously to Marian when they were finally ready to give their order.

No! she gasped, real alarm snapping her eyes wide. And don't *you* dare.

He held up a hand in surrender and smiled, hiding his surprise.

Later, while he waited between courses for Marian to return from the bathroom, he noticed the sister, Marta, serving at another table. As the manager had said, they were identical apart from the scar, even down to the way they tied their hair.

Marian seemed to get off to sleep much earlier that night: the light under her door shone for a while but soon he heard the creak of her bed and then, within moments, the snick of her lamp switch. He listened on for a few minutes, then went back to his novel. Before sleeping he went to the door and peered out across the yard. In two of the caravans light still seeped around the borders of their skimpy curtains.

Shortly after midnight he woke to a tapping at the connecting door.

Startled and dazed he called out *What? What is it?* more harshly than he intended and the tapping stopped abruptly. For a moment he wondered if he'd dreamed it. But there was the light again under her door. He sighed, threw back the covers and padded across the room. Marian, he called, more gently now. Marian?

She drew the door inwards, opening it just enough to show herself. She hadn't put her spectacles on and without them her naked white face looked long and vulnerable.

What is it? he said, whispering, as if there were someone else close by, still sleeping.

I can't get to sleep. My legs are aching. And I'm scared.

He stood thinking for a time, still waiting for his head to fully clear. You're just stiff from riding, maybe, he suggested. Come through to my room, anyway. Come and talk to me here.

She followed him through and perched herself on the narrow armchair facing his bed. Hamilton got back under the sheets, covering his bare legs. Are you warm enough like that? he asked, eyeing her pyjamas. They were undersized on her long limbs.

She nodded.

So, what were you scared about, honey? Do you want to talk about it?

It seems silly now, she admitted, and folded her thin arms across her middle.

Hamilton waited.

Well, she said. I felt scared because we don't know where the husband is. Or the two boys in the photographs. I told you it was silly, she added when he didn't reply.

But why's that scary? he said at last.

She shuddered and tried to smile. I don't know. It just seems really sad that they're in the photographs but they're not here now, and nobody knows where they are.

To his surprise, Hamilton saw she was close to crying. She held her face very still, as if frightened to spill the tears.

Well, sweetheart, he said, just because *we* don't know doesn't mean nobody knows. I'm sure they're safe and sound and very happy somewhere.

She nodded carefully.

If they weren't, she wouldn't put the album out where everyone can see, would she? If something bad had happened, she wouldn't want strangers looking at it and maybe asking her about them, would she?

She was absorbing what he had said, and it seemed to have worked, Hamilton thought. She sat back in the chair, already more relaxed, though her arms remained folded.

You think you'll sleep now?

I don't know. Not yet, she said.

Don't make me read a bedtime story, he joked, and was amazed to see her face light up at the idea.

Will you? she asked.

He groaned comically. No, honey. All I've got is some trashy thriller. Unless you brought anything?

No, she said. But whatever you've got is fine.

No, honey, I don't know. It's for adults. I'd have to skip over the racy bits.

That's okay, she said, though he couldn't tell if she meant it was okay to skip them or okay to read them anyway. He felt flustered.

I tell you what, he said, have a little glass of wine instead. I'll have one too and that'll help us both sleep. How about that? Have you had wine before?

Of course, she said, flustered herself now. I quite like it.

Good, he said. Everything in moderation. He winked at her and got out of bed to open up the mini-bar.

Don't tell your mother, he cautioned as they touched glasses in a mock toast.

She smiled nervously and sat back in the armchair. Will you read me just the start of the book? she asked.

He laughed. I thought the wine was *instead* of a story.

She didn't answer.

Alright then, he said, reluctant but flattered, and secretly pleased. The first chapter was tame enough, anyway, so far as he remembered. He reached across to the bedside table and retrieved the thick paperback. Here we go, he said, and self-consciously began.

Apart from a few expletives there was nothing to censor except for the chapter's last few paragraphs. When he reached them, Hamilton tailed off sheepishly and said: then some adult stuff happens, honey, and that's the end of the chapter.

Violence or sex? she wanted to know.

The second one, he said, a little taken aback.

Oh. Well I'm not a *baby*, she complained, but good-humouredly. She had finished the wine and at least now, he observed, she had the colour back in her cheeks. She looked fine, in fact. Her arms were unfolded, resting easily on the sides of the chair, and her eyes were shining.

Enjoy that? he said.

Mm, she said, nodding.

For God's sakes don't tell your mother, he warned again, getting out of bed and taking her glass along with his own through to the bathroom. I'll wash away the evidence in case the maid sees, he joked, and thought about Beata as he swilled the glasses in front of the bathroom mirror. When he returned, Marian had made no move to go back to her room. He climbed back under the covers.

Were you popular when you were at school? she asked him.

Why, sweetheart? He smiled quizzically at her.

But were you?

He laughed and shook his head. That's a long time ago. I don't know. I suppose so. I wasn't *un*popular. I don't think I was, anyway.

You remember Gabby?

Gabby?

You know. My best friend from home. You met her that day last year.

Oh, *that* Gabby. I remember, he lied.

She likes you.

That's nice, he said, amused.

She thinks you're *gorgeous*, she mocked, fluttering her eyelashes and swinging her knees open and closed like a shutter.

Oh really? he laughed.

She pulled a face at the thought of it. Even though you're older than anyone else's father, she said.

They were both quiet again for a while.

So who's *your* boyfriend? he asked.

She shook her head. Don't have one. I don't care, though.

That's right. There's plenty of time for all that, he murmured, then fell quiet again. Suddenly he felt sad. It was a strong, physical feeling, like tiredness after long heavy work. He wished she would go to bed and was sorry he had given her the wine. Come on, sweetheart, he said at last, let's get you back to bed. We've got lots to see tomorrow.

Where are we going to go? Her voice was drowsy now.

Let's see what the weather does.

She stood up unsteadily, putting out a hand and holding onto the chest of drawers at the side of the chair.

Easy, honey, said Hamilton, and got up swiftly to steer her through her door. He waited while she settled herself under the sheets. If you feel sick, wake me, he told her. She reached blindly for the soft toys on her bedside table and clutched the dog by a hind leg, dragging it to the pillow. The skin on her knuckles was angry and cracked. He hesitated, then stooped to kiss her forehead before turning off the light.

Back in his room he switched off his lamp before moving to the door and checking one last time on the caravans. They were dark too, now. In bed he lay flat on his back and waited for sleep.

★ ★ ★

Without the alarm to wake him Hamilton slept past nine and even then lay a while, wondering what time the girls came to clean the rooms.

After dressing he went through to Marian and shook her gently out of a dead sleep. How do you feel? he asked.

She stared up at him blankly, still turned inwards and lost, her dazed eyes big and dark. I'm okay, she mumbled finally, but only after he'd asked her a second time.

Time to get up, he said, faintly unnerved.

She nodded blankly and he left her.

Outside, one of the twins was hanging washing on the line whilst the other watched and talked to her from the steps of the end caravan, her arms crossed under her breasts. They both wore their work clothes. The day was fine and at last the Cairngorms were visible on the blue horizon, though the sharp peaks seemed weirdly trivial in the plain morning light. Hamilton waited for one of the girls to catch sight of him, then waved before strolling behind Marian to the dining room.

On the recommendation of the manager they spent the rest of the morning at a highland wildlife reserve. It was good for them both, Hamilton thought, to be properly high up at last and to feel the cold, thin difference in the mountain air.

At noon they climbed to a large wooden shelter overlooking the wolf enclosure. The timber all around them was roughly sawn and stank of creosote. Below them, a single wolf was visible, lying on its side in the sun, sleeping. Hamilton sat on one of the big, simple benches ringing the circular platform. Marian stared down into the enclosure for a while longer before joining him.

The whole platform's on stilts, she said.

Did you see the wolves?

Just that big lazy one.

You wouldn't want to fall down there, though, even if he is lazy.

She didn't answer. Do you think it's a wolf or a she-wolf? she said eventually.

It's hard to tell from up here, honey. The sun was hot on his face and he closed his eyes, enjoying it.

Is it true that sometimes she-wolves have brought up human babies?

He opened his eyes a crack. Where'd you get that idea?

There's that story about Rome. And the wolf-girl. That film about her.

I think it's just myths, honey. I don't know about that film.

It was based on a true story.

Oh, he said. Well, I don't know then. Maybe. He closed his eyes again and when he tilted his face back up to the sun he felt the irises pinch behind the lids. He heard Marian get up and clump around the platform.

It says here they're maybe going to put wolves back in the wild, in the Highlands, she called to him from the other side of the shelter. He looked, squinting. She was reading a board nailed to the central pillar.

Hamilton nodded. He approved, he thought.

To the east, a scroll of white clouds had appeared on the back of a freshening breeze. Even in the sun-trap of the shelter Hamilton could feel the new wind raising goose pimples on his bare forearms. Let's go down and see the wild cats in the cages, he said, down in the woods.

In the afternoon, after lunch in the village, he took her walking along the back road to the barracks. To begin with he had thought to show her the path along the burn, hoping to surprise her with the other river. What would she think, he wondered, when she saw it seeming to flow the wrong way and so much wider, and suddenly dark? But Marian's face when she'd woken that morning was still vivid in his mind; the pale head lolling when he shook her and the strange, deep senselessness swimming in her eyes. Somehow, the memory made the thought of any other strangeness repulsive, and he said nothing about the burn, even when she commented on the footpath, noticing it from the road. The barracks, stark on the hill, seemed a more wholesome place and, as they marched on, it was pleasant to feel the road begin to steepen and climb away from the marshy valley floor.

While Marian explored the battlements, the broken stairways and living quarters, Hamilton sat near the gatehouse, watching her. The buildings were simple and roofless and there was no mystery to them as far as he could see, but she seemed to be enjoying herself, wandering from one empty shell to another, observing. Behind him, an American couple bickered quietly at the gate before creaking open the thin metal bars and entering the gravelled yard. Overhead, the white roll of clouds he had noticed at the wildlife reserve had unfurled steadily westwards to cover the whole sky. Now they seemed to be lowering, closing in for rain. He called to Marian and waved her back to him.

On the road down they passed three low, bothy-like cottages advertised as holiday lets by a painted board in the nearest of their small front gardens. On the way up to the barracks Marian had paid them no attention but now she stopped at their shared gate. We could have stayed there, she said.

They're nice, Hamilton said. But the hotel's nice, too, isn't it?

She nodded.

We'll come back some time and stay in one of them, if you'd like that, he said. But she was already walking on and if she replied he didn't hear it.

That evening Marian called her mother again and then asked if she could join Hamilton in his room, though once there she seemed as reluctant to talk as ever.

Maybe Beata's saving up for plastic surgery on her lip, she said finally after a long period of silence.

Hamilton grunted and looked up from his book. Maybe she's not that worried about it, he said. It's very faint. What would it feel like, he thought suddenly, to run the tip of his tongue along the thread of it? He shifted on the bed. And anyway, he went on, you said you didn't think it made her look ugly.

I don't, she said, and left it at that.

Did she put your soft toys together again today?

Marian shook her head. I'll make coffee, if you want, she said.

When she eventually went to bed Hamilton slipped outside. It was early enough for the girls to still be waitressing and the caravans were deserted, their curtains wide open. He felt an almost irresistible urge to cross the courtyard, stealthily, and peer through each of the dark windows in turn. What would be the harm, when no-one was at home? He could feel sweat soaking his palms and the hairs on the back of his neck prickled as they rose. He stepped back inside and locked the door.

★ ★ ★

In his dream he was lying on the floor of a modern, spacious hotel room. The room was many floors up, he sensed, and he was staring at a pristine blue sky through one of its tall plate glass windows. The feeling of height and limitless space was dizzying and he was glad to be lying flat and secure. Then suddenly it was dusk and a huge owl, white and silent, the size of a man, alighted on the outside sill of the window. Its white flat face stared through the glass at him, and with a feeling of amazement Hamilton saw it was holding a large cat in its talons: a wild cat with pointed ears. He understood the owl had come from hunting over great snowfields and ice sheets and a feeling of awe, more at this sudden awareness of vast, blank silences than at the giant creature itself, gripped and paralyzed him. Don't let it in, he cried out, but now Marian's mother was behind him in the room and she moved calmly to the window to slide it open. Under the owl's huge, impassive face the talons relaxed and the wild cat dropped like a dead weight to the carpet. For an agonizing time it lay motionless, coiled, as if stunned. Then slowly and smoothly it stretched itself and rose to its feet, revealing itself now as a fully grown tiger. Bright as a flame it padded across the room to him.

Hamilton woke, his heartbeat frighteningly quick, eyes dazzled by the early morning light in the small, east-facing window. He'd forgotten to draw the curtains, he realised. Of course: that was why he'd dreamed. He rolled onto his wet back, blinking, still half stunned, then glanced at the bedside clock. It was just five but he knew he wouldn't sleep again now. The adrenaline from the dream was draining away but he felt a quiet, creeping dread, not relief, in place of the panic. Peeling the covers back, he sat himself upright on the edge of the bed. The low sun was staring directly into the room, and a vague memory of Stone Age tombs built to trap the sunrise played across his mind. A visit to Orkney, he thought, when he was Marian's age, or younger. His mother's mother had lived there. What a journey that must have been: even further north than this on the roads of fifty years ago, his parents, his two sisters and himself all jammed into a small blue tin can of a car, and then crossing the water to the islands. Now he could remember almost nothing of it, not the journey and not his grandmother. Most of life just happens and disappears, he thought. People and places, days and years all sliding into the dark, as if they'd never been. The old woman died soon after and they never went back. It would be the same for Marian, this holiday, he thought, in years to come. He needed to see her, he realised, and crept to the connecting door.

Marian's room, thickly curtained, was shadowy and the air was stuffy. She was lying sprawled, face down, breathing heavily. One lower leg, its pyjama covering rucked up to the knee, protruded whitely from the tangled mess of sheets. In the flat half-light the naked calf and the long, narrow foot at the end of it seemed oddly smooth and lifeless, like a spindle of bone. Hamilton had a sudden urge to wake her, just so that she'd turn and draw the strange peg of her limb back under the covers. But then what would he tell her? What reason could he have for waking her? He had nothing to say, just as he'd had nothing real to say all through the holiday. There was never anything to say, he admitted to himself now, and this longer time together had just thrown him deeper into the same old helplessness. All he could feel was a vague, powerless fear for her, and he didn't know how that could help or teach her at all. Was that love? he wondered. A kind of wordless dread underneath everything. Is that what makes us cling to one another? He couldn't even do that properly. The night before, when she was drunk, had been the first time since she was an infant that he'd even kissed her goodnight. All he would ever be able to give her now was money, or what money could buy. With a feeling of nausea he thought of his gift, the riding jacket, hanging empty and stiff in his silent flat. It was her loneliness he couldn't bear, he thought suddenly; at the station, in her own weird circle of stillness; and when she wore the jacket, pinched up in its newness, and her bony wrists and hands, her long, raw fingers, exposed, as if even the parts of her body were separate and lonely.

He wished he could sit on the bed without waking her. He felt unsteady, as if his thoughts were spinning him, physically. He was glad she would be going riding again today. It gave him time to gather his thoughts. Maybe he would go back to the game shop in the village. It had felt very peaceful there for a while, in the serious, musty, chapel-like quiet. It was restful to be amongst useful things, well-made, in their darkwood racks, all their purposes clear. He tried to picture the long sleek hunting guns and lacquered salmon rods more clearly but instead found himself imagining Marian riding in thick pine woods, through curtains of fine rain, part of a grey, silent procession. He frowned. Tomorrow he would take her all the way to the station in Edinburgh, stopping only to collect the jacket. He would give her plenty of spending money for the journey back and for weeks to come, and she would thank him awkwardly, mumbling as she took it, another packet of folded, deathly dry notes. This would be their last stay together, he was certain.

She stirred in her sleep and he flinched away, frightened at the thought of being discovered there, standing over her in the gloom. He retreated, shutting the door softly behind him.

After showering he lay on his bed thinking about his own parents, long dead, until it was time to wake her.

As they stepped out together to cross the cobbled yard they both caught sight of Beata coming towards them, her arms filled with neat folds of white, freshly laundered linen. It must have rained heavily at some point during the night, Hamilton saw with surprise, because the bright, rutted yard was gleaming with puddles. Over Beata's head, high in the south-west, a half moon was still visible, very pale but detailed with faint bluish shadows. She was hurrying across the uneven ground, clearing each little pool she came to with quick, graceful skips. Morning, Hamilton called, and Marian waved, and the hurrying girl fluttered her slim fingers back at them.

They spoke very little over breakfast. Marian fished at her cereal, leaving most of the milk behind in the bowl. At least she was washing her hands less now, Hamilton reflected, watching her stirring the spoon listlessly, though her sharp knuckles were still pink and chapped.

I'll go and settle the bill, he said finally. You finish up and then wait for me in the sun room, okay?

Okay, she agreed, and immediately slipped away.

Hamilton watched her disappear through the dining room doors and then fished a generous tip from his pocket, pinning the notes under the butter dish. His arms felt strangely heavy lifting the dish and placing his crumpled napkin beside it on the table. As if he were moving in slow motion, he thought vaguely.

The Reception desk was empty and nobody appeared when he rang the bell. There were voices drifting from one of the side corridors and he wandered along a dim, windowless passage towards them. The smell of detergent and stale laundry began to fill the air and soon he was at the half-open door of a harshly lit, low ceilinged utility room. The voices were closer now but muffled by the churning of washing machines and dryers and the clatter of crockery being sorted and stacked. He recognised the voice of the Scottish waitress, and then Beata's, or maybe her sister's, he supposed – the room seemed to be L-shaped and the speakers were hidden from sight.

There was a sudden burst of laughter, from the Scottish girl, he thought. Then, poor scarecrow! he heard Beata say, as she joined in the laughter. He stopped in the doorway and strained to hear. He caught the word grandfather amidst a jumble of fragments and then Beata must have moved nearer, or one of the loud, throbbing machines must have finished its work, because the words were suddenly clear. Anyway, these legs are worth watching! she insisted cheerfully. And he'll leave a big fat tip. And Mother of God, I'm telling you, men are just beasts, and always after the same thing everywhere.

# MY TEETH IN HIS MOUTH

With the students finished for the summer and with it being Friday and the middle of a New Jersey heat wave, Jesus closes the record store early. Hey, Robbie, he calls down the aisle, bumping through the front door with a box of second-hand stock, lock up and clear the register. He slams the door shut with his hip. Coming up the aisle, his pointed silver-toed boots clack like goats' hooves on the tiles. He dumps the box down on the counter in front of me. Go on, baby, lock up, he says. No-one's dumb enough to shop in this weather. He turns, squinting back along the aisle towards the big plate glass windows at the front of the store. A bright orange poster in Jesus's handwriting says:

¡AY, QUE PADRE!
New CDs
from
JUST $5!
&
VINTAGE vinyl!!

Apart from that, the big panes are empty. We both stare at the back of the poster; me, because my eyes are following his; him, I don't know why. The reverse letters are easy to read with the sun lighting up the paper. He turns the background music off and the afternoon traffic-roar rolls in with the sun. Tomorrow, clean the windows, man, he says.

While he waits for me at the counter, I go and lock the door. All along the aisles the sunlight flashes off the racks of CD cases.

You cool about losing the hours? he says when I get back to him.

I shrug.

Let's go in back, he says. I got somethin sweet'll make it up to you.

In his office he throws a Ziploc bag bulging with grass onto the desk. Fresh from my brother in Jalapa, he announces, and slides it open. This, *mijo*, was raised from original Acapulco Gold stock, he tells me. Acapulco fucking *Gold*, man – the legend. He takes a long, deep whiff before digging into it. The heat's even more stifling in the little back office. I'm sweating bad. I can feel it soaking my vest and shorts but Jesus in his usual black jacket and white shirt and skinny black tie looks dry and cool. He pauses from loading the papers and smoothes both hands over his long grey hair, tightening the knot of his pony-tail.

Heat like this makes the hit more intense, he tells me. Heat like this, it thickens up the fluids that carry the high; the delivery system. He licks along the double length of the joint, then scoots his chair back, swings his fancy boots up onto the desk and crosses them at the ankle. For a sixty year old hippy he looks pretty sharp, like a gambler in a Western, or a marshal. That's why it's always best to smoke in a hot climate, he goes on, wagging his Zippo at me. He lights up, takes a long deep draw and holds it a good while before releasing. It's more natural, he sighs out with the smoke. That's why God made *yerba* grow best in hot places.

Back through in the store the bell rings. We stop to listen and the door rattles hard.

Leave it, he says, but waits a few seconds, listening, before handing me the spliff and carrying on talking. You Scottish got beer. God gave you a cold wet high for a cold wet place, right? Children of the sun got *yerba*. I got Zapotec blood, *mijo*. The papery skin around his eyes creases up and he laughs without making a sound.

I cough a bit and nod.

He takes it back from me. Man, you disgust me, he says. You're sweating out your fucking *lips!*

By the time I get out onto the street the high's hitting like a hammer and the sun makes it worse. A truck horn blares right next to me and I realise

I'm veering off the sidewalk. A cop perched on a mountain bike stares at me from across the street but then pushes off into the traffic. I decide to take a walk down to the rowing club boat sheds. A couple of times I had luck there the summer I arrived. Apart from twinking at the pool, it was the first beat I found.

At the top of Main Street I cut towards the woodland walk which runs from the back end of the campus all the way to the riverside. Even though it's July a few students are still around and using the path – the usual jocks in training, drumming up dust when they pound past, an Asian couple walking ahead of me, carrying library books. I overtake them just as we pass the married students' quarters and they veer off to the big concrete building in the trees. I can hear small kids playing in the woods nearby, but they're nowhere to be seen.

At the river I sit on the lawn in front of the boat sheds, watching a family cooking at one of the communal barbeque grills. The smell of it comes over strong to me and after not wanting food all day I'm suddenly weak and shaky from hunger. The painted notice on the boat shed says DON'T SWIM. I close my eyes for a while and try to centre myself, but the bright red letters of the notice stay there behind the lids and I have to open them again to wipe out the image. Though the sun's beginning to dip towards the treetops on the far bank, the heat's still fierce. Just a few kids are paddling at first but then a young guy about the same age as me, in shorts and a university vest, wades out and takes a stand thigh-deep in the water. There's something familiar about him but I can't think what. He stares across the river, and lifts one arm to shield his eyes. The vest rides up under his raised arm and I see a big, flat pink scar the shape of a smile. Some kind of burn. It runs from just above his left hip to the middle ribs. Then I realise where I've seen him before – lifeguarding at the public pool. He drops his arm and turns to look my way. He doesn't make any sign but I can feel my luck building. The kids in the river are noisy and splashing around but the lifeguard's far enough away not to be bothered by them. I get up, kick off my sandals and step in.

The water's warm and cloudy. I stay close to the shed and watch him out the corner of my eye. He's ready to come over to me I can tell, but now the shallows start filling with other waders. Soon I have to back away from some old, grinning bald guy with his lapping Alsatian. All around my knees the water's covered in spent gnats, all spread-eagled in the surface film. Once I notice them I realise they're plastering the whole backwater, great spreads of them like a broken skin.

Then, maybe because of the grass still working on me, or the dazzle of the sun, or all the clouds of mud being stirred by everyone, I could swear there are things in the water, living things, Christ knows what, sliding round my legs and feet. My heart starts kicking like a horse. With all the mud stirred up it's impossible to see what's down there in the soup. I look up and fix my eyes on an empty spot in mid-stream, trying to calm my brain. The river's flat as a strip of tin. It's so wide and slow-moving there's no way of telling which way it's flowing. There's no way of knowing if it's going anywhere at all. I try to think about how long it would take to be carried all the way to the ocean, and then I get a thought about that big river in India where they put their dead, but the name won't come and all I can think is why do they do that? Then the sliding feeling comes again around my legs, like fingers, and a cold sweat breaks all across my back. I lift each leg, one after the other, nearly falling right over, a few broken fly bodies sticking to the hairs. I know I have to get out of there. I splash back to the bank faster than I mean to and drop onto the lawn. A fat guy lounging nearby says, sharks, buddy? but I don't pay him any mind. I strap my sandals back on and watch the lifeguard again. My whole body's shaking.

Hey, Francis, some guy calls from just behind me, and the lifeguard lifts a hand to greet him. Behind him, flashing off the water, the big low sun is blinding. I don't turn to see who's calling him. Francis, I say to no-one.

The next morning I call Jesus early and tell him I'm sick.

You lying son of a bitch, he says, still sleepy. What kind of sick?

Don't know. Could be the heat.

Could be the *heat*? Listen you lazy motherfucker, he says, it's Saturday morning. I need you there. If you're not there behind that fucking counter when I come by at ten, don't bother coming back.

In the background I can hear a woman's voice and a baby crying. He says something in Spanish away from the mouthpiece.

Okay. Well, so long then. What about the keys? I say.

Mail them through the door, you lazy fucking gringo. He puts the phone down.

I'm waiting outside the pool when it opens at seven. Already it's hot enough for the girl in the booth to have a little electric fan going. She doesn't smile when she hands me my rubber bracelet.

This early, the pool's almost empty. I watch a gang of old folks, three men and four women, lower themselves carefully in and launch out on their morning exercise of a few slow, calm lengths. It's restful to watch them. The water looks very blue, like the sea in a postcard, but I know that's just how the concrete under the water is painted. There's no sign of Francis. Another lifeguard – a round, red-headed girl – jogs out from the changing rooms and climbs the platform. She keeps a close eye on the old swimmers, frowning thoughtfully at them. The air stinks of chlorine. I rub in a handful of sun cream, cover my face with a fold of towel, then lie back and doze.

There's noise all around me when I wake and I realise I must have slept for hours. The sun's already high and even before I move a muscle I know I've been burned through the sun cream. I sit up painfully, my stomach scorched. Behind me a young girl is talking. Just say yes or no, she says.

But I don't know. I don't know if I do or don't.

Well yes or no? I have to fill in *something*.

I still don't know.

If I don't fill in anything it won't work. There's no box for 'don't know'.

Well that's lame.

I twist onto my stomach so I can see them: two pretty little mall rats in shorts and crop-tops. One of them, a skinny blond with bobbed hair, is hunched over some teen magazine, her pen hovering over a page. Her Latino friend, plainer and dumpier, is propped back on her elbows, frowning over her shades. They don't notice me at all.

The blond girl sighs. When we add up the numbers it's all going to be wrong. We might as well not have started.

It's only one question.

But it throws the whole thing out.

I guess. The Latino struggles to sit upright. She plucks at her crop-top and then lies right back. Just put down no, she says, talking to the flat blue sky.

Can't you decide for real, though?

Okay, put down yes, she says.

The blond winces and taps her pen against her straight white teeth. I'll put down no, she says after a while. If you don't know, I think that's more accurate. She marks the page, then stares all about her.

A whistle blows and I squirm round to sit upright again. It's Francis. He's on the opposite side of the pool, jabbing a finger at two boys horsing around at the pool's edge. No you don't, he mouths; no-you-don't. The boys trot away from the water, grinning.

I don't know, the blond girl says behind me. It's too hot to think about stuff anyway.

Add up the scores, though, her friend tells her, her voice weird and hollow-sounding suddenly, like she's talking in a deep sleep.

The other girl groans.

If you don't add them up there's no point.

I watch Francis making his way slowly round the pool's perimeter. The old folks are long gone and all the lanes are crowded with random, splashing bodies. Just about every step he takes, pool water slops over his feet. Everything's glittering.

A tall, black-haired woman pads towards me, dripping from her swim. She catches my eye and hitches up her soaked costume. She passes close by and I hear her flap out a towel next to the two girls.

Having fun? she says.

Sure, the blond girl replies. It's too hot though.

I hear one of them rummaging in a bag and then the gasp of a ring-pull being peeled back.

You still doing that questionnaire?

Uh huh. The adding up part now. It gives you a score.

Is it about boyfriends?

No. It's about 'Are you ruled by fate?'.

So what's the difference? she teases.

Oh mom, the Latino drones, her voice still dead as a stone.

Francis is close now, passing right in front of us. As I stand he turns and gives me a puzzled look, then a quick smile of recognition. Hey, he says quietly, and carries on walking. I dive as well as I can, ball up underwater and watch all my silver breath pour out of me. When I surface, he's watching. I fall away into a back-stroke.

I swim till I'm tired out, then drag myself up one of the chrome ladders and head for my towel. I've lost sight of Francis but the girls and the woman are still there. All three of them are shading their eyes and peering up at the sky.

I lie back, stretching myself flat out, every muscle weak and trembling, and realise they're watching a micro-glider circling high up above the town. Soon it wheels into the sun and I lose it in the glare.

He's just going round and round in a circle, the blond girl complains.

It's just like a big paper airplane, says the mother.

Why doesn't he just come *down*? the dark girl says, but nobody answers.

I can hear my breathing, like the air's scraping the walls of my chest. Tiny and high, the glider swings out of the sun again.

Hey, says the blond, what if he had, like, explosives tied to him and was looking for something to fly into?

Hush. That's not funny, sweetheart, the Latino's mother replies.

Well Pastor Parks, he said Arabs could buy nuclear bombs now which would be small enough so you could like carry them in a baby buggy, and it would be totally worse than 9-11.

Yeah, the Latino girl broke in, like it was a baby. To fool people and get into places.

What's there to blow up here? the mother says, and stares up again at the tiny circling figure in the sky, shading her eyes. Anyway, how about we think about something a little happier now?

But that weirdo up there, he could carry something like that in his arms, the blond girl insists.

But how would he steer? the Latino says.

Maybe that's why he's going round in circles, the mother says tartly, and the blond girl giggles.

At closing time, Francis stays behind on trash duty. I leave, circle the block, then he lets me back in. He takes me to the walk-in store cupboard, snaps the light on and locks the door. I sit myself on a wholesale carton of Clorox and peel off his damp trunks. You'd better put this on, I say.

Wait, he says, and everything stops except the blood knocking in my head. You just being cute, or pos?

Pos, I say.

Shit! he whispers. Any second I expect him to pull away, but he doesn't. He stands there, not moving a muscle. I can smell the chlorine trapped in the flat coils of his hairs. Okay, he says in a tight voice. Put it on. Then he says something else I don't catch, and I can't say anything.

The next day he skips work and we get drunk in his apartment watching re-runs of *Bonanza*. He tells me he's starting a PhD in philosophy and looking at the stacks of heavyweight books all around the apartment, I believe him.

How'd you get that scar? I ask him, in between episodes.

He laughs and shakes his head.

I'd like to know more philosophy, I tell him.

He laughs again. There's philosophy and there's philosophy, he says.

We avoid the other subject for most of the day but in the end he says: so how long has it been?

I tell him I found out last fall.

What you taking?

Can't get anything, I say. I'm not supposed to be here.

He snorts. So go home. Get treatment there.

I like it better here, I say. This is home now. Anyway, I feel fine.

Christ, he says, and goes to the fridge for more beer. When he comes back to the couch he's shaking his head. He hands me a tin, then moves away to sit in the armchair opposite. You don't feel anything yet?

I don't know. I get pretty tired some days. But I think I always did. It's hard to tell.

It could be years before it shows.

That's what they said.

Hm, he says, and chews his lip. Well, man, any of us could go any time. None of us knows when, I guess.

That's right. That's my kind of philosophy, I say.

You should go back, though, he says, still serious. You're fucking crazy not to go back. You can get retros and all that shit for free in the UK, right?

If I start to feel it I'll go back.

You should go before the winter comes in. Once you get sick you'll need looking after and shit. He narrows his eyes, like he's examining me. You can't get help around here, he says, then sighs. I don't want to talk about it, he says.

Me neither.

He squints at me again and runs a hand over his hair. Listen – no more fun, okay? It's freaking me out. He opens his beer and takes a few long, loud gulps.

Okay, I say, but later he asks for it anyway, so long as I'm careful.

By Wednesday I've got my job back at the record store. The first few times I call, Jesus puts the phone down, but in the end he lets me speak and ends up taking me back with another pay cut. Listen, he says. I'm hanging my dick out giving you work without a card. No more games. You got that?

Okay, I say.

Okay. See you at ten, he says. He sounds tired.

That Friday the weather breaks at last and turns to rain. Jesus pays me part cash, part Quaaludes just arrived from Jalapa. You know, he says, no-one up here even knows about these babies any more. No-one even knows their name. It's a tragedy, *mijo*. Me, I'm old school. He rattles them in their canister. Like a slow ride down the river, man. *Padrisimo*. He tells me there's a storm blowing in, coming up from Virginia.

I take the Quaaludes round to Francis's place. He's heard of them, he says, but never tried them. You shouldn't be taking this shit, he says, but we drop a couple each with beer and settle down for the evening. It's peaceful in his little apartment with the piles of deep, meaningful books everywhere, the smell of fried chicken from some other apartment and the sound of the rain beating down outside. It's early twilight and looking at the grey window I wonder if we'll spend the fall like this. The thought makes me feel kind of sleepy and comfortable.

I need to study for the next few days, Francis says suddenly. I need to catch up. I'm meeting with somebody from the faculty next week to see if they'll enrol me.

Cool, I say. I kick off my shoes and set my bare feet up on the couch.

Listen, Robbie, he says, but then just shakes his head and goes on reading his book.

For a while I sit staring at the window, watching the rain tap and run on the glass and the dark filling in the sky behind it. The sunburned skin on my stomach is itching so I peel off a few dead strips and roll them into scrolls.

Don't do that, Francis snaps, seeing me drop some of it onto the floor.

There's a wind getting up outside. I can hear it in the scrub oaks. Earlier in the evening, while I was waiting for Francis to get home and let me in to the apartment block, I saw two black squirrels chasing each other under the trees. They were smaller than the usual grey kind. I never even knew squirrels could be black, but there they were, chasing around. Maybe the change in the weather made them nervous. I look at Francis in his chair, reading. Every now and then he underlines something or scribbles in a notebook.

Don't watch me, he says. Watch TV or something.

It won't bother you?

No, he says. Then he tilts his head and rolls it from side to side on the back of the chair. Those ludes, he says, they're taking hold of me now. He blinks hard and stares up at the ceiling, showing the whites of his eyes. I can't stop reading the same fucking sentence, he says. I finish it, and then it's there again, where the next one ought to be. He looks back down at his book and laughs kind of miserably to himself.

I turn on the TV. Leeza's talking. She introduces a new guest and the audience start clapping and hooting. The guest is some earth-mother type woman, big as a bus, dressed in a long white kaftan. She walks awkwardly, like her hips are damaged. At the bottom of the screen the words WORLD-RENOWNED MEDIUM keep flashing. The studio sofa's too little and low for her really and she doesn't look happy seating herself down.

They get talking and the medium tells Leeza that the spirit world flows all around us, two feet above ground level. She says that on the spirit side, the TV studio is the site of a great temple. There are spirits, she says, passing in and out of the temple.

What, right *through* us? Leeza wants to know.

That's right! Right through us, she says, eyes popping wide.

In the audience, hands shoot up. I would like to ask the lady, a young black guy in a Bulls vest breaks in, why do they need a temple? I mean, if they're already in the afterlife?

Someone starts to clap but stops when nobody else joins in.

The big lady leans forward, eyes screwed up. The need to worship is not a *fleshly* need, she tells him.

The young guy nods and shrugs. Okay, he says.

She turns on the rest of the audience. This is not more real than the temple, she scolds, waving a puffy finger at everything round about her. This is not more real.

I look at my bare feet laid out on the couch, big and cold and white at the ends of my legs. I can move them but I can't feel them. I lift one onto the other, heel to toe, trying to picture how deep two feet is. I think from where I'm lying it'd be over my face. Over my mouth and nose and everything.

Listen to this, Francis says, his voice slow and slurring. 'To say I think he is in pain is like saying I think my teeth are in his mouth.' He stops and looks up from the book, staring at me, like he's waiting for something. That's Wittgenstein, he says.

Oh. That's good, I say. My teeth in his mouth. I like that.

He laughs into his book again.

When I shut my eyes my heart feels like it's swaying instead of beating. Just a slow, swinging bag of blood, bumping against the ribs. I think about it bursting and the blood coming loose, flooding me. The medium's still talking but I'm having trouble sorting one word from another. In my head I'm back at the river, high up, circling really slow, round and round, just like the guy above the pool, looking down at everyone – Francis, the old man with his dog, teenagers hand in hand, kids paddling – all fixed there under a big, blazing sun. The brown river looks smooth and still but I know it's moving. I feel sick with fear. I need to shout a warning, but I don't know what about, and no sound comes anyway. It's something about the river moving, but it's something and it's nothing – just panic. Just a kind of dread. Their faces are all turned up to me, white and tiny. Even if I could shout, they'd never hear a word.

Francis, I say, forcing my eyes open, what's that river where they put all the dead?

What? he says. He peers at me, squinting hard, like the sun's right behind me for real. The Styx?

No. A real river. In India.

The Ganges, he says. And it's just the ashes, ya dumb mutt. He shakes his head at me. And listen – don't start with that morbid shit. He rubs his eyes with the palms of his hands. When he stops, he stares at the TV. There's a strange, ill look in his face.

Right here, the medium says. Right here is a temple.

Turn that off, he says. And listen, Robbie, he says, for Christ's sakes go.

# RAIN

It must have been rain that brought the pigeon down – a sudden, furious April downpour that overtook and drenched Ahmed just as he drew close to home. He had bowed his head into the wild drive of it, a fusillade of water and stinging hail pounding the bulging shopping bags that swung from his numbed hands.

Indoors, as he dried his head and changed his clothes in the bedroom, he listened to the rapid march of the storm passing over and fading. By the time he got to the kitchen to unpack the groceries the wind was already drying the garden outside. A low, late afternoon sun, free of clouds now, was casting a watery, unconvincing sheen across the lawn. The grass was still sprinkled with white peppercorns of ice and in the midst of them stood the pigeon, motionless and cowed, as if stunned. Slim and pale, almost white, it was clearly not one of the wild scavenger pigeons his wife often tossed bread into the garden for. It was a racing bird, Ahmed decided, noticing the tin band on one leg and the blue plastic ring on the other. He lit a cigarette and watched the bird for a while. Every time the wind gusted and swirled its feathers ruffled along its back and nape, but it made no attempt to find shelter. It seemed oblivious to his movements behind the window.

The next day, a cool, blustery Saturday, the bird was in the garden again. Ahmed stared from the kitchen window as it strutted tamely behind Rana when she went out to fill the long tubular bird feeder she had hung on the garden shed half way through their first, shockingly cold, Scottish winter. Taking up position below the feeder it picked at whatever seeds were spilled by the squabbling sparrows and finches.

Ahmed pointed out the pigeon as Rana stepped back indoors. Did you notice? he said. It was here yesterday, too.

She nodded. It belongs to somebody – it's tame and there's a number on one of the leg-rings.

He sipped his coffee. It's either lost or resting.

She agreed and washed her hands, then left the kitchen.

Ahmed stayed at the window, watching. He opened it a crack and the sounds of the garden filtered in on chilly air: the cheeping of the sparrows at the feeder and, when the wind rose, a thin whisper in the bare branches of the nearby trees. More pigeons landed clumsily beneath the feeder. They jostled a little and the racer gave ground to them but in general the heavy, slate and cement-grey city birds seemed indifferent to the smaller visitor. A sharper gust of wind set the trees hissing and with a slapping of wings the high-walled garden emptied.

Over the next week the bird was an almost constant presence in the garden, either patrolling under the feeder or simply standing alone and still in the middle of the neat square lawn, as if lost in thought. Just before dark it would disappear to roost somewhere in the near gloom but each morning it was back, unafraid when they entered the garden, but growing more wary with each day if they drew too near.

Towards the end of the week they noticed its left foot was growing lame. From the window they could see the clawed toes bunched arthritically and as the days passed it moved around under the feeder with an ever more obvious limp.

Though he kept it to himself, this new development bothered Ahmed. When Rana was out of the house he indulged a growing interest in the bird and would sit the back step to observe it, smoking and keeping watch for the neighbours' fat tomcat. It also occurred to him that the lameness might draw the attention of the other pigeons. From the same kitchen window he had once wasted an afternoon watching a crippled blackbird in the garden, one foot a simple, toeless peg, being harried to exhaustion, and no doubt death in the end, by its own kind. And another worry was the rain. When it fell heavily and the other birds found shelter the racer, bewildered, hunched on the lawn as it had that first day, easy prey for any cat or hawk, if hawks hunted in Scottish rain. And underlying all this, more unsettling somehow, was the sense of hopelessness, of doom even, that these occasions evoked in Ahmed. The strange docility of the bird, its passivity, seemed awful to him, so much so that once he stepped out himself, arms waving under the beating rain and tried to scare it into self-preservation. Reluctantly, it hopped to the far end of the small garden but refused to fly. Disgusted, his thin house shoes already soaked through, Ahmed let it be and hurried back indoors.

We should try to find its owner, Rana suggested on the second weekend. It can't still be resting, and it's going lame. We could try to read the number on its leg.

You try, said Ahmed. It knows that you fill up the feeder. It's used to you.

He watched from the window as she stalked it, slowly and patiently, crouching low, her back to him. Like a big, shy bird herself, she cocked her head, poised and still, close enough now to reach out and touch it if she chose. Instead she backed away, still crouched, then straightened and wrote on the back of her hand. She stood watching the bird for a while longer until, impatient, Ahmed tapped the glass.

Who will you call? he asked when she came back in.

There's a royal society for birds. I'll get their number.

A royal society?

They might want to come and rescue it, she said, ignoring the derision in his voice. She watched for his response.

He shrugged.

She turned to the window again. I think the band on his leg is too tight. I think it's cutting off the blood. I don't think I could catch it, though, to take it off.

No, he agreed.

She went through to the living room and soon Ahmed could hear her voice, formal and halting but, as far as he could tell, very correct. Whatever she was arranging seemed to involve more than one call. He lit a cigarette and opened the door into the garden. Their pigeon was still feeding alone on the ground though above it quick relays of sparrows were flitting to and from the feeder. A crow had perched on the ivy-strewn back wall of the garden. It watched him as he smoked with something like intelligence, or at least curiosity, Ahmed thought.

After a while he sensed Rana behind him and half turned his head.

They gave me the number of the pigeon club it came from, she said. I had to phone the secretary and he gave me the owner's number, so I called and spoke to him. He sounded nice. An old man, I think. She was speaking rapidly, still flustered. Ahmed knew it was a great strain for her to speak and listen over the phone. It tested her English to the limit. He wondered if he should have offered to do the phoning for her, but instantly decided he would have felt too absurd. Besides, the garden and the birds were her interest, her domain. And using the phone to speak to strangers was exhausting for him too.

He said he'll come through from Inverness on Monday evening.

Inverness? All that way?

She shrugged.

Does he expect us to catch it?

No. The man says he can do that if it hasn't got too wild yet.

It's not wild yet.

It's getting more shy, though. Every day.

But it's not wild yet. Look at it.

They stared as it limped amidst the husks and seeds, remaining calm even when the other birds scattered at sudden shadows or shifts in the spring breeze.

The man says it's a young bird and they can turn wild quickly.

We'll see, he said doubtfully.


The next day, very early, Ahmed watched it feeding as usual but by the middle of the morning it had disappeared and he saw nothing more of it through the afternoon and short evening. Rana too was clearly looking out for it more attentively than usual, and as it grew dark he saw her scatter a handful of seed over the middle of the lawn before collecting the washing from the clothesline.

On the Monday it was back but hopping, awkwardly – perhaps with exhaustion – rather than limping.

Don't watch it all day, Rana said when she came downstairs to find him. You have to get some work done.

I know, he said, stung, but when she left for her classes he carried his books through to the narrow breakfast bar in the kitchen and settled to work there in sight of the garden.

When he stopped for lunch he decided to sit a while outside with his cigarette and coffee. It was a cool but bright, windless day and the bird, when it wasn't feeding, seemed content to sun itself on the low roof of the garden shed. Ahmed carried out one of the tall bar stools, returned for his cup and cigarette and then perched himself on his high seat, enjoying the sun on his hands and face. He thought about the arrival of the bird's owner later that day. It was a long drive from Inverness, much of it through the highlands, he supposed. They had never travelled any way other than south from Aberdeen in their eight month stay but he imagined vaguely the north and west as a sunless, grim landscape this early in the year, its narrow roads hemmed in by giant, naked flanks of rock and scree. He pondered what method the old man might use to capture the bird. The closest he had seen Rana get was on the day she had noted the number on its leg-band. It would be less trusting now, he suspected. He let his thoughts run on for a time as he finished his coffee and cigarette, then took his empty cup indoors. The pigeon was still settled on the shed roof, awake but basking. He would test how wild the bird had become, he decided. He would see whether its lameness, surely critical now, made it more wary or more resigned.

From an open bag in one of the kitchen cupboards he took a fistful of birdseed and carried it out into the garden, moving slowly across the lawn towards the shed. He held the seeds up to the bird, catching its attention, then furled his palm to a funnel and poured them in a thin trickle as he backed away, laying a short trail in the grass. Then, squatting on the balls of his feet, he waited, a few seeds still sticking to the moisture on his open, upturned palm.

Soon, the long muscles of his thighs began to burn. The bird, after stirring a little at first, now seemed sleepily indifferent again. Ahmed rose, his knees cracking. Here, he said, self-conscious at the sound of his voice in the empty garden. He moved forward, arm outstretched and with a sudden, soft clatter of wings the crippled bird launched itself and flapped swiftly out of sight over the roof of the house. For a moment Ahmed froze, then slapped the last of the seeds off his palm and went back indoors.

At four, when Rana returned home, Ahmed said nothing about scaring the bird. It still hadn't returned, he knew, but when she came through to the study to tell him so he widened his eyes, as if surprised.

That poor old man, she said. I'll put out more seed.

There's still time, he said.

She hurried back to the kitchen.

Soon after six he answered the doorbell to a heavy, crop-headed elderly man and, half hidden behind his bulk, a much younger boy of sixteen or so. The youth was pale and skinny and a flat fall of long brown hair narrowed his face even more. Ahmed offered his hand and the older man, after a moment's pause, took hold of it, grasped firmly and released.

You're here for the bird? Ahmed said.

Aye. The loon here's my grandson, ken? He helps me out with them. The old man seemed to be focusing on a point just beyond Ahmed, as if distracted or unwilling to meet his eyes. It unnerved him until he guessed that Rana must be at his shoulder.

Hello, he heard her say, shyly.

Ahmed made room for them to enter the hall, backing into Rana. He turned his head to follow the man's gaze and realised he was staring at his wife's head covering.

Eh, the man said to her, from your accent you sounded French on the phone, ken? I thought you must be French.

Oh, she said, her mouth still smiling, yes we can speak French. She darted a glance at Ahmed.

The man grunted, his own big-featured, square face relaxing a little. Aye, well.

Come in, anyway, Ahmed interrupted, and ushered them through the hall and living room to the kitchen.

The youngster, Ahmed noticed, was carrying a small cardboard box in one hand and a dirty white plastic tub in the other. He wore a loose black T-shirt and on its back was a timetable of dates and places. *Slipknot European Tour 2003*. The numbers were drawn as if they were frayed lengths of rope.

At the back door Ahmed slipped past them both and unlocked it to let them through into the garden.

Would you like tea? Rana asked, hanging back on the threshold.

Aye, said the man. Just a droppie milk. Thanks.

Aye, thanks, said the boy, blushing faintly when she turned her eyes to him. Milk and two sugars, please.

The early evening air was cooling rapidly after the fine weather of the afternoon and there was no sight or sound of bird life. Even the sparrows had abandoned the feeder. Ahmed looked up at the sky and saw that just a narrow band of tired blue remained in the west above the roof of the house. The sun had already dipped behind the tiles. From the east a cold colourless emulsion was spilling slowly across the city skies. The air was oppressively still.

It's not here for once, he said. He made a show of scanning the nearby rooftops. It's normally here until dark.

The man grunted. I can see fine why she settled down here, right enough. He gestured at the bird feeder. Fond of the birds, aye?

My wife, said Ahmed. She has an interest in them.

Aye, well well. He followed Ahmed in surveying the sky and the roofs all about them.

The young boy wandered towards the centre of the lawn. She might be roosting nearby, like, he said and shook the tub a few times. It was full of seed.

Aye, well, give us that then, the old man said and went over to him to take the tub. He walked to the back of the garden where, beyond the ivied wall, a cluster of hawthorns, nameless shrubs and crab apple trees had been allowed to run tangled and wild. Coom on, he urged, up at the empty branches. Coom on. He rattled the tub slowly and rhythmically, *shuck – shuck – shuck*. After a while he crossed the length of the garden and faced the near gable of the house, staring up as if the bird might be hidden behind the chimney pots. Coom on then, he called, and again jolted the tub.

If she's close enough to hear that she'll come down, the boy explained.

Ahmed nodded, watching the old man's heavy, deliberate movements, his big steel-toed boots, soiled cardigan and slack workman's denims. Already he was impatient, jogging the tub more sharply, clearly wishing it could all be over and done with. The boy was still peering hopefully at the tops of the scruffy trees beyond the wall or turning on his heels to scrutinize the wide, blank skies and deserted rooftops surrounding them.

Rana came out with the teas and the old man gave up shaking the feed while he sipped at his mug.

No sign yet? she asked, pained.

The grandfather shook his head. She's been here every day, though, aye?

Oh yes. Every day. For about two weeks. She glanced at Ahmed for support and he nodded.

Aye. Well well. He squinted up at the last streak of blue in the sky then lowered his face to the steaming mug again. They go wild, see? he said. Feral, ken?

There was quiet for a while. A lone gull swept into view and took up station on the high roof of the Catholic school at the head of the street. They all watched it settle. As if following its lead a scatter of pigeons hove into sight before circling away back towards the heart of the city.

Your bird's a fine looking pigeon, said Ahmed. Quite different to the wild ones.

It was the boy who responded. Aye, he said with feeling. Most racers are just blues like the wildies. Nothing to rest your eye on.

Ahmed smiled at the youngster. Yes, he said. Nothing to rest your eye on. He relished the phrase for a moment. Are your birds valuable? he asked, turning his face to the grandfather.

Oh aye, he answered quickly. They were my brother's birds to start with, ken? He had a triple bypass and wisnae allowed to keep them for a long whiley after that.

Too sensitive to infections, the boy added.

Yes, said Ahmed.

But he didn't want to just get rid of them, ken? the old man finished.

We've lost quite a few this year, eh granda?

The man grunted.

Lost fifteen to start with on the Alloa race, eh granda? Only three of them ever got back, like.

Fifteen? Ahmed repeated, shocked.

Aye, well maist of them young birds, ken? the grandfather cut in. Like this one now. Inexperienced. Disnae take much weather to bring them doon, ken? And the weather that week was gey fierce.

What happens to them? Rana asked.

Both grandfather and grandson shrugged. Some rest up and get home days later, like, the boy said. Some of them get killed off or go wild and some of them join up with other flocks of racers out getting trained. Then they get taken in by the owners, like.

Valuable birds, ken? Mind, some fanciers'll get in touch and see you get your bird back.

Aye, the *decent* ones, the boy intoned in an oddly sombre voice.

Again there was silence while the callers sipped at their tea.

If it doesn't show this evening I'll try to catch it tomorrow, offered Ahmed, unsettled by the turn the conversation had taken. There was something depressing about the old man's detachment in the face of his losses. It was confusing, too. Why had he bothered coming all this way for one lame bird when the next month he might lose another dozen and react to it with nothing more than this fatalism? At least the boy had some feeling for the things. Some enthusiasm. The exchange had left Ahmed feeling rebuffed, and somehow exposed. He cleared his throat, wishing he knew of a courteous way to bring the whole futile episode to an end. His offer to catch the bird seemed to have met with silence but then the grandfather spoke up.

Aye, well, I'll leave you the feed here and the box. If you can get close enough you might be able to grab her.

To grab her?

Aye. Be quick. You won't hurt her, ken? He signalled to the boy who handed over the small box they'd brought with them. It was branded Fed-Ex and the lid folded somehow into a basic cardboard carrying handle. There were air-holes in each side and a printed warning that shipping should not exceed forty eight hours. She'll be fine in there for a whiley, the old man said. It's designed for pigeons, ken?

I'm sorry you've had a wasted journey, said Rana. It must take hours. She stared pensively into the sky. The high cloud cover had thickened and darkened already.

Well well, the old man murmured. Eberdeen is where we cry from originally, ken, so it's nae too bad. He nodded towards the boy. The loon here was born at Forester Hill. The infirmary, ken?

Oh really? she said, brightening, but Ahmed noted that she didn't mention she sometimes worked there.

Three dark pigeons appeared over the roof line and landed, scuffling for position on the slope of the gable.

Wildies, said Ahmed, and as he spoke a sudden fat drop of rain plashed on the left lens of his spectacles. In a moment the air was filled with the quick ticking of water striking the rooftops and ground around them. Bowing their heads like pilgrims they filed indoors.

Two days passed before the bird returned and Ahmed had all but given up on it. He was standing on the back step, smoking in the sunshine, enjoying what felt like the first truly warm morning of the year, when it flapped down, clumsily, to its usual place under the feeder. It could hardly stand now and half-hopped, half-lurched from seed to seed.

Slowly, Ahmed stubbed out his cigarette, edged indoors and found the white tub of corn and grain left behind by the old man. Shaking it with the same slow rhythm the grandfather had used he advanced on the bird, crouched low, murmuring self-consciously: coom on; coom on. The bird stopped its feeding to observe him. Gently, he reached into the tub and scattered an offering of grain. There was a long, still pause, then it hopped lopsidedly forward, pecking at the seeds, almost within reach. Coom on, he urged, and rested the tub on the grass between his knees, freeing his sweating hands. He lunged, but without conviction, and the bird escaped easily to the roof of the house.

Ahmed straightened and turned towards the kitchen window. Rana was standing behind it, frowning anxiously. Don't watch me, he said, loud enough for it to carry through the glass. She turned away and busied herself at the washbasin. *Just grab it*, he thought with some bitterness, though he knew his nerve had failed him. At the last instant he had flinched back from contact, hadn't closed his hands as if for the kill but had jerked them forward, uselessly, as if shooing it away. It was the injured leg, he reasoned to himself. Part of him was fearful of damaging it further. But he knew that really he had dreaded the prospect of contact. He had never handled a bird before and had always, even as a boy, hated the sensation of an insect or any other living thing cupped in his hands. The frantic batting of a trapped moth on his palms repulsed him and always lingered on the nerve endings long after he had disposed of it under Rana's watchful eye. It was a petty but somehow shameful weakness that he liked to think Rana was completely ignorant of.

The sun, almost at its full height now, was unseasonably warm. Ahmed sighed and with his sleeve wiped the sweat from his forehead. The bird seemed calm again and unlikely to fly off, at least. It watched him from the safety of the gable.

As he entered the kitchen, Rana said: You'll need to be quicker than that.

Ignoring her, he took a chair from underneath the dining table and carried it outdoors. He collected the tub of grain from where he'd left it on the lawn and sat on the chair facing the bird, the sun beating on the back of his neck.

After a while, from the garden next door came the sound of a door opening and children's voices, a boy's and a girl's, spilling into the mild air. Home for their lunch, thought Ahmed, and found the idea oddly calming. Soon, the *pok* of a tennis ball on concrete punctuated their conversation. Their accents were too broad and their chatter too quick and muffled for Ahmed to follow much more than a few phrases. Then the father, home too for some reason, warned them to 'move away from there, now' and they bickered a little over who should move where. A sudden stink of drains – puzzling – wafted to Ahmed. An opened manhole, maybe. An unblocked gutter? The smell faded again and the father spoke more cheerfully to the children, teasing them about something before going inside and thumping the door shut behind him. Ahmed frowned, but the bird seemed not to notice. Soon the boy and girl were quarrelling again. *One more time*, the boy warned, in a cross, shrill voice, *one more time...*

After a hurried lunch Ahmed saw Rana off to the college and then returned to his vigil. The children from next door were back at school – they had passed him, hurrying and giggling at some shared joke as he closed the front door behind Rana – and the garden was peaceful. Perhaps because of that, the bird was feeding again and reachable.

This time there was no mistake. A trail of corn and grain brought the bird almost into his lap where he knelt, patient, for several long, uncomfortable minutes. He was better balanced this time, and all the force of his will directed the simple, smooth movement that pinned the creature under his trembling, wet hands. One wing he managed to clamp tight to the body, the other had already sprung open for flight and now projected at an odd, quivering angle. He hugged the body close to his chest, trapping it there, while he adjusted his grasp and folded the wing flat again. Then, still kneeling, a cold wetness chilling his knees from the soft ground, he stared at the bird and took stock, elated and a little stunned by his success, his sudden mastery. There was no resistance from the thing in his hands: a faint warmth reached his fingers from beneath the flattened spines of its feathers but no quiver of panic or struggle. His first flush of triumph ebbed away and Ahmed wondered at the creature's apathy. Upending it, he inspected its crippled leg. Still there was no reaction, no twist of the neck to find and stab at his fingers. Ahmed could make nothing of the balled foot. Other than being curled unnaturally tight, the sharp pink toes looked healthy enough. The plastic leg-ring looked secure but not constricting. Righting the bird again he rose painfully to his feet.

Indoors, he lowered the bird into the Fed-Ex carton and half-secured the lid, folding the cardboard tabs loosely enough to allow a narrow view of the white head and nape bobbing and shifting in the dark of the box. He watched the bird for a while, again struck by its calm acceptance, then left it alone to call the old man.

There was no reply and no answering machine. When Rana arrived home he tried again, and again every hour or so throughout the evening but each time the phone rang on without reply.

Leave it, Rana said at last, exasperated. You can try again tomorrow.

Where is the old fool? said Ahmed.

It's late now, come to bed, she said, her calmness irritating him even more.

You go. I'm checking the bird, he snapped.

Deep into the night after hours of restless, dream-filled sleep, Ahmed was woken by rain battering at the window. He lay hunched, his shoulders knotted and aching, listening to its loud, gusting fall. The warm, summery promise of the day before seemed absurdly distant, a memory of another season altogether, another country. His chest, like his shoulders, was painfully tight and his pyjamas, wet with night-sweat, clung to his arms and thighs like bandages. Twisting to lie flat on his back he gasped and stared up into the dark. He put a hand to his heart and with his fingertips massaged the hollow of bone there. Rana was snoring gently at his side but no part of her body touched his. Time passed so quickly here, he thought, season to season in a kind of windswept turmoil. And his work progressed so slowly. His mouth was parched.

He had been dreaming about the holding centre where, after entering the country, they'd been separated and held for a day and a night while their stories and papers were checked and cross-checked. At the time, still dislocated by long travel, he had accepted it all with tired resignation. The officials had been cold but not aggressive and when he wasn't being questioned he'd been allowed to kill time playing chess, rustily, with a glum, middle-aged, overweight, Algerian doctor. The Algerian claimed to have been invited to a medical conference in London which had begun and ended during his detention, but beyond that complained very little. Privately, Ahmed hadn't believed him: his pale suit had been shabby and his teeth were very bad, though he played chess well enough to beat Ahmed easily in every game and had, impressively, guessed at heart disease in his family after just a casual inspection of Ahmed's clumsy, overlong fingers as he moved the chess pieces. It had occurred briefly to Ahmed to test the man's story himself, but then he had thought, what difference did it make to him? He had enjoyed his brooding, gloomy company; had been fascinated by him, in fact.

You know, my friend, the Algerian had said, inexplicably using English instead of Arabic or even French, you know the latest research in my field shows that the heart doesn't simply wear out with age. He'd glanced again at Ahmed's hands. The cells of it, they are triggered at some point, you understand, and they cease to renew themselves. They simply cease. That is the truth. He'd paused to play his move. And the other vital organs, too, he'd added, and gestured vaguely at his own rounded trunk. They are trying to explain this finding, he'd said. But they are scientists so it makes no sense to them how a living, beating thing of muscle, without thought or feeling, can somehow choose to stop living. How? he'd asked in mock amazement. Then he had wagged a curved, fleshy finger at Ahmed. But it's no mystery, my friend. He had widened his puffy, baleful eyes, fixing Ahmed with his gaze. Allah chooses, he had said. The will, and the hand, and the eye, they are disobedient. But the *heart*, he had finished triumphantly, even in its cells – *that* is obedient.

Ahmed had smiled and nodded, not knowing what to say.

The first dreams he'd had of the holding centre all involved the Algerian and had left Ahmed feeling thoughtful and sometimes confused, but with no strong emotions. In them, the doctor was garrulous but cryptic and Ahmed's dream self quickly became tangled in long, intense dialogues, the trailing ends of which lingered on as teasing, surreal puzzles after waking.

This night's dream had been different, and darker, though Ahmed could remember very few of its details. The Algerian had been there to begin with, but had been replaced by, or had become, some kind of interrogator. Ahmed could remember none of his accusations and questions, but knew they had filled him with humiliation and rage.

To calm himself, he tried to fix his mind on the bird and the satisfaction of capturing it, but that too seemed to lead him only into a web of weakness and defeat. He saw it dazed under the rain and felt again its unnatural, deathly lack of fear when trapped in his hands. Even a spider, even a mindless fly would have struggled more.

Rana groaned at his side and suddenly it occured to Ahmed that the accuser in his dream had been the bird's owner, the old man. He strained to recall more details but nothing came. Instead he found his thoughts drifting to the old man's brother, whoever and wherever he was, awake like him, maybe, flat on his back in the dark with his butchered, makeshift heart. He moved his palm from his chest and breathed deeply, closing his eyes. Where the weight of his hand had been a vague pressure remained as if a great, shadowy finger had found him out and pinned him there. He was sweating again and knew he had to move. Rana woke briefly as he slid from the bed and he heard her murmur her older sister's name. Then she was lost again in sleep and Ahmed padded quietly out of the bedroom.

In the kitchen he made himself a strong black coffee and lit a cigarette. Part of him expected the bird to be dead and he shrank back from checking its flimsy coffin. Instead, he opened the back door and finished his cigarette whilst staring out into the garden. Somewhere in the darkness gulls were quarrelling. The earlier rain had passed over but the wind was still squalling and in the east a faint bar of light revealed the underbellies of rank upon rank of rolling storm clouds. From one of the back bedrooms of the house next door an electric light shone but there was no other sign of life and the weak, cold glow was cheerless and somehow unwholesome. The coffee was bitter but warming and he drained the last of it before tossing away his cigarette butt and stepping back inside.

Now, finally, he went to the box and eased open the lid. The delicate pale head was already cocked to meet him with a wakeful stare. Its eye, just a few inches away now, regarded him, but without feeling or intelligence, Ahmed was sure. It glittered with life but was hard and depthless; just a tiny, bright black mirror. A soft tremor of sound seemed to ripple in the bird's throat, but so briefly Ahmed wondered if he'd imagined it. Turning its head from him it tapped with its beak at the cardboard wall in front of it, but without urgency. Was it standing, or sitting to protect its injured leg? The walls were too tight to its body for him to see. In the gloom of the cramped box the colourless head dipped and swayed.

New rain was spattering at the kitchen window and above him Ahmed could hear Rana moving on the upstairs boards, awake and anxious, dressing to search him out. His fingers were cold and cumbersome and he fumbled to fold the lid.

# WHERE I LIVE

It was midday, end of August, and for one last time I was riding the Amtrak north out of New England. I had a letter I needed to write, things that needed to be said, and I was thinking I'd have more chance if the guy two seats back would just shut the hell up a while and let me think straight, let me hear what I was trying to say. He'd wandered into the carriage an hour before – a skinny, thirty-something red-head with a scrap of beard, dressed loose and carrying an army stores pack like he should be hiking some trail, not riding the Boston to Burlington commuter line. He made his way to the seat behind me where the young girl was sleeping and joined her. When she woke he started talking in his low, sleepy monotone, hardly waiting to hear her answers.

Where I live, he was saying now, we get trains passing through maybe once, maybe twice a week. Way up country, that's the way it is. It's pretty lonesome. But pretty peaceful, too. He paused. I guess it's both.

The girl must have been about thirteen or fourteen and I'd wondered what she was doing alone, but she looked neat and clean and well-cared for. It wasn't my concern. Other than us, the carriage had been clear and I'd taken a good look at her sleeping when I boarded. Long, straight blond hair; cool, pale doll's face; doll's hands. So still, you wouldn't think there was breath in her body, let alone a baggage of words.

I don't think I'd like that, she replied.

No, he said. I guess you might not. You like the country, though?

Mmm, she hummed, like she didn't want to say.

You don't like the country?

No, she laughed, embarrassed.

I love the country. I couldn't live anywhere but the country. You really don't like the country?

No, she said again, sounding a little discomforted now. I don't like bugs and stuff, she apologised.

Oh I get it now, he said, his tone brightening. You're right not to like the bugs, he said. He whistled a single trailing note. Where I live, the bugs sometimes, they can eat you alive.

I'll bet, she agreed, happier again. I know what that's like from camp and stuff. When I was a kid.

You know, you'll probably think this is kind of gross, he went on, but where I live, in the summer, we don't use deodorant or anything. I mean we wash and all. But nobody wears deodorant because it draws the bugs. But I don't know – you probably think that's gross, right?

She said something but it was too quiet for me to hear.

The worst ones are called deer-fly, he said.

There was a long silence then. Maybe a minute or more.

Jeez, it's quiet in here. Isn't it quiet in here? he said at last. You notice that? You notice how empty the train is?

Uh huh, she said.

After what happened last week, with those planes and all the craziness, all the people in the cities, they're living in fear. No-one wants to ride a plane or even a train now. That's my theory. Where I live, you won't get that same kind of fear because it's a city thing.

I guess, she said.

You watched it on TV? You saw it all happening?

Uh huh.

You saw those guys jumping?

She said nothing, but I imagined her nodding.

He whistled a single, trailing note. Amazing thing, he said wonderingly. You and me, he said, we're kind of like refugees from all that, on this train. Or like old pioneers. Everyone else, they're too scared to move. They're all huddling together, because of fear. That's my theory. But you and me, we're on the move. We're on the way out of all that craziness. We're heading for the big old empty spaces, right?

Then there was some sort of rummaging and I remembered the canvas kit-bag he had with him. I wondered what he was looking for. See that? he said, and she let out a giggle. Hey, he said, you know how I'm a red-head? Well red-heads are supposed to have something called a recessive gene. You know what genes are?

Uh huh. We studied those.

Well you know how with dogs you get, like, leader dogs and pack dogs? Well a recessive gene means you're a pack dog. But me, I'm kind of a leader dog. So I figure I'm, like, a mutant or something. It's like I'm the exception that proves the rule. You ever heard that phrase?

She asked him if he had a dog.

No, he said, but where I live is good country to keep a dog. Hey, he said, you know that joke, the one that goes 'it's in your jeans?'

No, she said, and he didn't take it further.

There was quiet again then and through the window I watched the hot late summer sun bearing down on Vermont. I put pen to paper but instead of writing found myself making the outline of a nude, reclining, slender limbs wide open. I blocked it off, filled the square with ink, turned back to the low sun and woods. The harder I looked, the more I seemed to see pathways winding through the trees, though I knew it was a trick of the light.

Just look at all those leaves, all ready to turn, I heard him say, and for a second I was startled as if it was my shoulder he was suddenly leaning at, my ear his lips were nearly brushing.

I stared at my hands; the smudged fingers, wet palms.

I love the fall, she replied, her own voice grown dreamier. When the leaves get really pretty – that's so neat.

I thought you didn't like the country, all that outdoors stuff, he teased, but gentler than he'd picked at her before.

Well, y'know. She giggled at herself, then thought for a time. You don't get bugs in the fall.

No, he said, slow and almost melodic. No – most bugs die.

I imagined him nodding as he spoke, his pointed beard dipping; I pictured her smooth, upturned face.

You know all these woods are famous, he told her. In songs I mean. Old songs about Vermont. You know that song, 'April in Vermont'?

I don't know, she said. They're nice though.

You like music?

Uh huh.

What kind?

Oh, I don't know. Lots of kinds I guess. I kind of like Christina Aguilera.

He let out a death-rattle and she laughed. Man oh man, you like her stuff? Really?

Yeah. Well kind of.

You like the way she is in that new video though? You know the one where she's dancing and her clothes are all like, sweaty and dirty and torn?

She hesitated. I guess it's ok, she said.

You wouldn't wear anything like that though?

I don't know. I guess not.

You like her though?

Yeah, she said. And The Smashing Pumpkins.

Oh, you like the Pumpkins? Okay. Cool.

She laughed again, shyly.

You like all these woods though?

Uh huh. I like these kinds of trees. They're not like, big dark winter trees.

You mean like pines and firs and stuff, right?

Yeah. The kind you get on mountains, in snow and all.

Yeah, he mused. Where I live, it's like this.

It must be nice, in the fall.

Oh yeah. You should see the fall up there. You know, you should just miss your stop and get off with me where I'm going and see it all for yourself for a couple of days. You could do that.

I don't think so. She laughed. But she wasn't uncomfortable anymore.

Well, I was just kidding. Where I live, I kid people all the time.

She didn't answer and I realised I'd started drawing again.

I'm kind of known for it, he said.

I closed my eyes, shifted away from the window where I'd been leaning. And maybe the sudden movement reminded him I was there in front of them, because he said nothing for a long while after that, even when she said something about a deer feeding at the tree-line.

After a time I opened my eyes and craned across so I could see clear down the aisle. We were almost at the tail of the long train and the far carriages beyond, where he came from, looked as deserted as our own. I considered moving on into one of the last cars, but something kept me sitting there with them, feeling the same rocks and bumps, waiting. I finished another nude, the same girl but standing this time, lewdly, and again boxed it, then scored it all black.

I dozed fretfully for what must have been hours, woke at a small station where no-one got off or on. The sun was much lower now, flooding in through the glass with a mellow, golden glow. Behind me, they were speaking again, but softly, as if it was already night. I knew then the words I had to write wouldn't come, not that day, and not ever. I looked at the few lines I'd written, signed them – though God knows they couldn't have made much sense – and folded the sheet closed. The nudes were still there, in their ink coffins.

All I wanted was sleep – sleep to the end of the line – and I wasn't sorry to hear him wander on back with her, still talking softly, too soft for me to understand, into the empty carriages.

# IN THE VALLEY

The track was closed to vehicles – she remembered noticing the sign – but something was approaching anyway. Every few seconds Laura saw the distant, unmistakable flash of a windscreen winking through gaps in the trees. Whatever the vehicle, it was moving slowly and any sound its engine made was swallowed up by the tall loose hedges and waving corn fields, all the heavy mid-summer growth nodding and whispering for miles around in the blazing Basque sunshine.

Finally it passed her – a battered grey Mercedes with a heavy, middle-aged man hunched at the wheel. Laura stepped off the track into a fringe of tall weeds. The driver nodded curtly when she raised a hand but he hardly turned his face to her. A chip of gravel sprang out from one of the rumbling tyres, flicking her bare shin, but the car was crawling too slowly to raise much dust. For a while she waited, watching it lumber away, then carried on. She knew it would have to come back the same way soon. The bottom of the dirt road, a mile or so down the track, was blocked except for the wooden stile she'd climbed and there had been nothing more than footpaths leading off from it. She quickened her pace.

According to her map she should have arrived already at Arizkun. The track was marked as a byway on the old Santiago pilgrim route and she'd taken it on impulse when she saw the symbol – a white scallop shell painted on the stile. She regretted it now: the walking had been much easier on the road. Here, down below it, the trees crowded in and the baked mud surface, rutted and braided with old motorcycle tracks, threatened to turn her ankles at every step. Even the swarms of flies seemed thicker, batting against her sweating face and following the trickles of sweat inside her vest.

Still, she told herself, pausing to hitch her backpack higher, the path was beginning to climb again now, and anyway it was good to be finally walking the valley, whichever route she took. She had meant to do it at least a week earlier – as soon as possible after arriving at Nerea's apartment in Elizondo. But the days since then had slipped by somehow, leaving Laura with the sense that she was close to outstaying her welcome and would have to set out on the journey soon, or never.

She blamed circumstance more than her own inertia for the delay. When she'd arrived, nothing was the way she'd been led to expect, and the effort of adjusting seemed to somehow steal from her all the emotional reserves she'd stored up for the walk. For one thing, Nerea was sharing the small second floor flat with a strange giant of a man. The boyfriend, who Nerea had never once mentioned to Laura in their months together as student flat-mates in Granada, was a glaring, blackly bearded truck driver called Mikel. Mostly silent, if he spoke to Laura at all it was in quick, incomprehensible Basque and as far as Laura could tell he never left the flat. They had sex very loudly at night too, the pounding and creaking always accompanied by Nerea's mercilessly detailed, full-volume commentaries, all of which first mortified Laura, then left her empty and restless for hours in the dark. And every day they spent most of the time wordlessly stoned. The dim living room, where they slumped in front of endless re-runs of natural history programmes, was a foggy, flickering den from mid-morning till four when, dazed and staggering, Nerea would finally raise the bamboo blinds with a clatter, throw open all the windows and try to drive the stink out before the first of her pupils arrived at six for English lessons. The first day of her visit Laura had tried to keep pace with them but by the afternoon they had to lay her flat on her back on the outside balcony until the nausea and anxiety passed. After that she simply kept them company while they smoked and that in itself was enough to make the days pass by in a dreamlike, timeless haze. She had told nobody she was there, not even her mother who always insisted on knowing every detail of her travels, tracing them on an old touring map of Europe, and no-one in Elizondo or the whole of the Baztan valley knew who she was or why she had come, and no-one cared. It was a quietly heady feeling and seemed to go naturally with the cloudy, weatherless atmosphere of the apartment.

Laura had told nobody, either, exactly why she wanted to walk the Baztan valley. She'd decided that she couldn't fully explain the impulse even to herself. All she knew was that since hearing of Calum's death just over a month ago – a car crash somewhere on the road between the riverside villages of Arizkun and Eratzu – her first numb shock had turned almost at once to fury (he was killed alongside a young local girl, just sixteen, and was drunk) and then, gradually, to an overpowering need to visit the place where it had happened. Maybe then she could make some kind of peace with him, not just over his betrayal but also her own: after learning about the girl she had ignored the funeral in Edinburgh, though her mother had offered to pay for the flights and she could have stayed at home with her just an hour's drive from the city. Weeks later, she discovered from a mutual friend that Calum had never told his family about her anyway, a fact that still tormented her if she allowed herself to think about it, but despite everything he'd been her first lover, the first boy who'd ever wanted her, as far as she knew, and for the first few months in Spain when they were both new to the country and adjusting to their student exchange years she was almost sure she'd meant as much to him as he had meant to her. After they'd made love for the first time he'd stayed awake with her for hours in his single bed, talking quietly, stroking her arms and breasts in the cool white light of the campus street-lamp outside the window. It was only when he transferred his studies from Granada to Pamplona that the doubts crept in. And then – almost immediately it seemed to her now rather than after the long, insecure months that actually passed – there was news of the accident and all her gnawing fears were simultaneously confirmed and ended, forever.

At last, and quite suddenly, the trees cleared and the scarred mud of the track gave way to a ragged crust of tarmac. She was at the outskirts of the village, the sun beating down overhead. A single old-fashioned diesel pump, caked with rust, stood off to her right and a tilting corrugated shed, its doors wide open, to her left. Someone was running a bench saw inside – she could hear lengths of timber being shrieked through, turned with a clatter and passed through again. As she drew level a leathery headed old man in blue overalls and dusty plastic goggles stopped his sawing to watch her, the circle blade still whining at full speed.

Arizkun? she shouted over the din.

He nodded and called something out to her in rapid Basque, then turned back to his work.

Ahead of her, between two large, red-tiled houses, she could see what looked like the village square. A church steeple rose above the rooftops there and she followed an alleyway towards it. Away from the clamour of the shed the village was wrapped in a deserted, drowsy hush.

A priest in his long black cassock cycled slowly past and turned into the shadowy cloisters of the church dominating the far side of the square. She heard him brake and dismount somewhere in the shade of the arches; a creaking door opened and slammed shut heavily after him. Behind a nearby slatted gate, tall and whitewashed, hens clucked and fussed. The afternoon air was very warm and still. She trudged on through the empty square towards the edge of the village where a wooden sign announced in both languages the road to Eratzu.

Walking the actual stretch of road at last, after weeks of imagining it, she realized she'd been assuming all along that the exact place of the crash would somehow be obvious to her. Vaguely, she had imagined a broken dry-stone wall, scarred trees or scribbles of tyre marks on tarmac. Now, looking about her at untidy hedgerows and wire fences she understood with a feeling almost of alarm that by this time there may be no sign left at all. The thought of having to ask about the crash at one of the farmhouses along the way, or even in Eratzu itself, unsettled her but she knew she'd go through with it if need be. She'd come too far now.

Gradually the road was climbing and the landscape opening out. On her right hand was a fringe of scrub trees but beyond them were gently climbing fields of pasture and finally, in the distance, high, heather-topped hills. In between the hills ran narrow green folds of spate valleys with here and there isolated farmhouses dotted on their slopes. To the left, a rough expanse of meadow fell steeply down to a line of pine trees a few hundred yards below. She supposed the Baztan was there, glittering behind them, but couldn't be sure. Near the pines a few cows were grazing, model-like in the distance, their bells tolling with a faint, saucepan clatter. A magpie rose up from a nearby fence post, startling her. It glided down towards the cows and disappeared behind the dark screen of pines. At intervals she passed bales of hay skinned with tight black polythene and despite their wrappings she thought that she could just catch the faint sweet stench of grass fermenting in the glossy drums.

She'd been told that the accident had happened on a dangerous bend but so far the road was running either straight or in gentle, sweeping curves. It was easy, peaceful walking: there was very little traffic to force her up onto the embankment and for long stretches she could put the purpose of the trek out of her mind and almost imagine she was strolling at home again in the Perthshire hills. After almost an hour she came to a sudden dip, the road falling sharply and bottoming out briefly at a narrow stone bridge before climbing just as steeply into a tight bend that vanished left into thick woods. Two farmhouses stood facing each other on either side of the hollow. Now, she thought, she was getting close. The road was changing – becoming less predictable – and she felt her senses sharpen with a mixture of excitement and dread. Slowly, studying carefully the low stone walls on either side of her, she made her way down to the bridge and then up the other side, but there was nothing. At the second farmhouse a baying dog flung itself at the tall palings, making her flinch and hurry on. She passed three neat, chest-high woodpiles and then the road plunged her into a tunnel of trees where the tarmac gave way to a sun-dappled surface of hard-packed, gravelly dirt. A fine white dust billowed up into choking clouds whenever the occasional car or camper van sped past and each careering vehicle made her heart lurch as she stepped back into the brush and made way for it.

She found the place almost within sight of Eratzu. At the foot of a high, ancient oak tree a fresh wreath and the remains of older, dried out bouquets lay amongst the massive tangle of roots. Above them a dusty framed photograph the size of a sideboard portrait was fixed to the trunk. She studied it for a while, light headed suddenly, then backed away and sat down heavily on a shelf of grass and bracken, still staring across the road. The girl in the photograph, dressed in what looked like some kind of school or church uniform of white blouse and dark blazer, was smiling brilliantly. A pin on her lapel, picked out by the camera flash, glittered against the sombre cloth. Only when a sudden car swept past, its radio blaring, was Laura jolted from the smiling image of the girl and back to herself. Her breathing had become so shallow she was dizzy. Through the trees she could hear the bells of the village church ringing out the hour. She counted three chimes. Still sitting, she eased the backpack from her wet shoulders and fumbled for her bottled water. With some surprise, she realized she was very hungry, though it was more a feeling of sudden, empty weakness than a real appetite for food. The warm water made her feel sick but she forced most of it down before packing it away again and struggling to her feet. She would need to eat or the vigil she'd planned would be impossible.

Just beyond the bend with the oak tree she found herself emerging onto a clear rise overlooking Eratzu. To the left of the road a neat graveyard lay ahead, fenced off by spindly iron railings. Opposite the gates, three blocky stone crosses stood waist-high, tilted and half smothered by bracken, on the side of the track. They looked very old, their edges rounded by weathering. Maybe something to do with the pilgrim way, she guessed. Underfoot, between the ridges left by tyre tracks, the dust was thick enough to cushion her sandals and sift hot between her toes.

At the heart of the village a triple-arched bridge straddled the Baztan. On its far side the bell tower of the church rose up to a tiled witch's hat whilst at the near side a heavy plank door led Laura down into a cool, dim cellar bar. A knot of locals and the tall young bartender were clustered together, staring and muttering at a soundless television mounted high in the corner. Laura glanced up in time to see footage of some kind of police operation with dog handlers and vans, then the screen cut to a newsreader's bland, mouthing face. The bartender detached himself from the group and moved along the counter to face her. He was irritated by something, she could see, and could hardly bring himself to listen to her. She ordered a small beer and four of the stale looking *pintxos* almost hidden in the shadows behind the bar. As soon as he'd served her he returned to the huddle of men beneath the screen. Some of them were bickering quietly now in Basque. Others darted sidelong, unreadable glances at her. The slices of chorizo were curled and tough as bark on the dry bread but with the help of the beer she steadily chewed each portion down.

As soon as she was done she paid and quickly climbed the staircase back into the sunshine. Walking the few steps onto the bridge she looked down at the Baztan. The water was low but dazzlingly swift and clear. Some evenings at the apartment, passing the time while Nerea was tutoring, she had stood on the balcony to watch the river at Elizondo. Sometimes Mikel had joined her and wordlessly flicked pieces of crust down for the ducks and trout. The water was much slower and darker down the valley at the weir pool. This didn't seem the same river at all. She turned away and crossed the empty street, heading back the way she'd come.

The graveyard gate was unlocked, just a heavy iron latch keeping it shut. Inside, she picked her way around the small family crypts that stood here and there amongst the graves like gardeners' huts of stone and marble. There were no caskets to be seen beyond the barred entrances but each tiny house contained a low altar at the back with a brightly painted, doll-sized plaster Christ crucified above it. On her way back to the gate she realized that almost all the graves, however simple, had stone panels at their feet and brass handles as if the tombs could slide open like drawers. She crouched to examine one of them, trying the handles, but the approaching rumble of a car leaving the village made her spring upright again, embarrassed at herself. Once the car had passed she hurried back out to the road, dropping the iron latch with a bell-like clang behind her.

There was space to sit comfortably on the embankment opposite the oak but not for her to sleep, as she'd planned. Instead, she pushed a little deeper into the bracken and found a clear patch long and wide enough to unroll her groundsheet. Returning to the side of the road she managed to collect an untidy fistful of wildflowers, intending to leave them alongside the wreaths already there. But when she brought them to the small heap of offerings and had to face the photograph again she suddenly lost heart. In the picture, the girl's dark, uncomplicated hair fell smoothly to her shoulders. Above the white teeth the wide-awake eyes were deep brown and warm, though the skin around them hadn't creased in keeping with the broad, confident smile. Shyness? Laura wondered. Or some other kind of falseness? Anyway, she was beautiful. Taking the flowers back into the undergrowth she scattered them furtively, filled with a strange sense of indecency and clumsiness. The half-thought of both Calum and the girl watching her movements from some other place, some other reality, teased at her imagination and she found herself having to thrust it fiercely away before it led her into terror.

As soon as it grew dark she crawled into her sleeping bag, feeling foolish and almost unbearably alone. There'd been no point in her vigil, she saw that clearly now. There was no more connection to be found with him here than anywhere else; she'd been crazy to think there might be. What was there to connect to? She felt sadness, almost overwhelmingly, but knew that it was much more for her own confusion than for Calum's death. Then, slowly and despite herself, she found her imagination turning to the girl, to the mild brown eyes she knew were fixed through the dark on her sleeping place. She turned her body away from the road and listened as an owl called from somewhere deep in the dry oak woods. Feeling tears welling up she wrenched herself onto her back, resisting them, gasping deep, fierce breaths.

The night was perfectly clear and finally, staring upwards at layer beyond layer of sharp, bright stars she found herself growing calmer and remembering the last time her mother had been in love. It had been at least ten years ago – just after the divorce, when she was still willing to date and Laura was still young enough to be sent to bed early. He'd been a married man, and all Laura could recall of the relationship now were the awful days of her mother's deflation and loneliness following the occasional late nights he spent at the house. She wasn't sure if they'd ever been lovers, though for years in her early teens she'd burned with curiosity about it, and sometimes found herself secretly ashamed of her occasional eavesdropping and imaginings. Now she couldn't even remember his name, nor his face or voice, though he'd always been kind and natural with her. What had happened to end it? Did her mother ever think of him now? She saw an image of her mother suddenly, not with a man and not ten years ago but poring over her map of Spain, its place-names and symbols, tracing where Laura had been and was supposed to be. Then, for a time, she succeeded in clearing her mind of everything except the small sounds of the night around her and the stars and the brilliant white disc of the moon rising over the black hills. But sleep was impossible and as her mind grew tired it seemed to slide beyond her control, betraying her with image after image of Calum, happy and triumphant, driving the radiant girl in the picture. Maybe he'd been driving the way he'd once driven with her, Laura, when he took her out of Granada high up into the cold, snow-capped Sierra: one hand lazily on the wheel, the other toying with the wet tangles of hair between her legs... And then she was lost – spasmed into a foetal curl, biting on the flesh of her arm to stifle the sobs and howls that surged like storm waves through her body.

She woke at dawn, exhausted and paralysed with cold, and it took her almost twice as long to walk back as it had to climb up through the valley. There was no reply when she rang the apartment bell though she knew both Nerea and Mikel were normally awake and smoking by now – it was nearly eleven. Suddenly angry, she shrugged off her heavy pack and trudged stiffly round the back to shout up at the balcony.

Eventually one of the other apartment doors burst open and Laura recognised Nerea's neighbour, a stocky, sullen old widow who was also the caretaker of the block, glaring down at her over the balcony rail. Wait! she commanded and disappeared back inside. Soon she bustled through the side gate into the garden. Gone, she announced before Laura had time to speak. Both gone.

Laura stared stupidly at the widow's broad, faintly triumphant face, almost too weary to reply. Where? she managed at last.

Mikel – Guardia. Nerea, who knows? She shrugged her big, rounded shoulders.

Guardia? Why? She thought instantly of the hash and felt a wave of relief at having escaped.

Again the caretaker shrugged. They question him. Very often. Always they release him. She raised her dark eyebrows and sniffed. They are pigs and fools. She regarded Laura intently, rolling her tongue around her gums. He is Batasuna, she added, as if as an afterthought, and snorted. *La política,* she said then, slowly and carefully, as if teaching a child.

Oh, Laura heard herself say, wrong-footed again. She recovered herself slowly, conscious of the old woman's heavy, impassive scrutiny. Will they let him go today? She felt dizzy and longed to sit down safely on the grass.

Today, tomorrow, two days – who can tell?

I have some things in the flat, Laura croaked, close to desperation. Some clothes and money. I'm very tired. Could you let me in for the night, or until Mikel comes back? We are good friends. He would trust me.

The caretaker seemed to ponder for a while, pursing her thin lips.

I've been staying with them all week, Laura added when the silence grew too much to bear. I've passed by you on the stairs, she added, almost pleading. You remember?

The old woman grunted, then gestured for Laura to follow her back into the building. She disappeared for a while into her own apartment before emerging to show Laura a spare key. One day, one night, she said, holding up a short, thick forefinger. No more.

Yes, Laura agreed. One night. Thank you.

All right, she said, and gave up the key.

The flat was as the Guardia had left it. The cushions were intact but ripped from their covers and strewn about the floor. The mattresses in both bedrooms were stripped and stood on end, sagging against the walls. On an impulse she righted the larger, double mattress in their bedroom rather than her own, flung herself down on it and slept dreamlessly through the afternoon.

By early evening the humid morning had given way to cool, driving showers. From the balcony during a break in the rain Laura saw a small stray cat, yellowish and painfully thin, crouching at the riverside border of the back garden, hunting water voles or frogs, she guessed. In the kitchen she found a tin of sardines lying on the floor where it had been swept from one of the ransacked cupboards. She emptied the tin onto a plate, forced her feet into Nerea's abandoned slippers and hobbled down into the wet garden. The cat had a blunt, ugly face, its mouth extending downwards in open sores at each corner. Its expression reminded her vaguely of the cowardly lion and even its skin was like a costume, sagging loosely off the bones. It was easy to lure. She scooped it up deftly to her chest, its breathing making a faint rough sound and giving off a whiff of decay. It was shockingly light to lift and hold. Indoors, it sniffed the sardines but would eat nothing except a few licks of milk from a different saucer.

Just before dark the rain closed in again. She was staring down at the weir pool from the balcony, watching for any sign of life, though nothing in the river was stirring. As the first big drops fell the cat writhed out of her arms and darted into the flat. Laura watched it flash away, faintly glad to be free of it, then turned back to the river. It was somehow disconcerting to think that the slow, dark water below had followed her all the way down the valley from Eratzu. The dusty streets, the bridge and the graveyard that had looked so much like a strange village all to itself seemed to belong to another world altogether now. And the river came from somewhere further back again, she thought, feeling the rain begin to soak her hair and seep through the shoulders of Mikel's heavy, musty bathrobe; came from somewhere in the empty Basque hills she'd seen from the road and watched from her camping place while the big red sun fell slowly behind them. She began to wonder how far, but it was impossible to guess and tiring to think about. And Nerea and Mikel. Who could say if they'd ever come back now? And who knew where anyone ever really was, anyway? Even when they were right beside you. Even inside you. Even that.

# A PIECE OF THE MOON

The Wednesday of the funeral I get woken by the doorbell. By the time I reach the door in my pants the doorstep's empty and all I can see is this big old white van parked a little way up the street. It looks like a busted up ambulance, but there aren't any signs. The driver's knocking at a door on the other side of the road from me. He's a fat man without much hair and he doesn't look too clean. He waits a while at the Protheroes' door, then pushes a slip of paper through it and moves up one. I look down and sure enough there's a yellow leaflet on the mat, blank side up. I close the door softly in case he hears and comes back.

It's too hot to get dressed so I pull all the curtains shut and go through to the kitchen. Everyone's already out to work or school, but there's a note left on the table. Wear this tie with your blazer, it says, and next to it there's one of my old man's black ties rolled up like a party horn. I get myself a glass of milk and take it through to the living room. I put the TV on and run through the stupid learning programmes like I do when I'm off school sick. I end up watching a guy at a table with a telescope, magnifying glass and microscope all in a row. He starts talking and touching them.

I go over to the window and put my head between the curtains. The light's dazzling. I look up the street, squinting, but the van's long gone. By now it's about nine.

On the TV the guy and the table have gone. Instead there's these big rough scale things, like slabs. You can tell it's through a microscope.

There's no voice, just violin music. I keep looking and the slabs get smaller and you get to see these tree trunks which you could guess are just hairs. The camera moves through them for a while, like they're a forest. Then, which is meant to be a surprise, you see this massive fly. It's in the middle of a bunch of hairs, stood over them like a dinosaur, except with its sucker going. It's putting me off my milk, but I keep watching. Then the view gets bigger again, zooming out, and you get to see the fly sitting on a patch of skin. Then, next thing you know, the skin is part of some kid's wrist, who's sitting in a boat on the sea. It's a sunny day there, too, wherever that is. Anyway, it carries on and soon you can hardly see him, just the white boat he's in, this little dot on the blue sea. Then not even the boat. Then it goes up and you're in space, looking at the whole ocean he was on, in fact all the earth and everything, and further out past the moon and other planets and stars. It's all bullshit, but there I am, still watching.

The guy's voice comes back and I walk over and switch it off. I feel like I should be thinking about Hooper, seeing as I was meant to be one of his best friends and it's his funeral in a few hours. But the trouble with thinking about Hooper is that he stuffed himself with pills, so they cut him open, and whenever I try to think about him that's all that comes into my head – Hooper all opened up like a fat white fish, on some cold slab. All his guts out and everything. So for the past few days I've stopped thinking about him at all. But Jesus, I'm thinking, you should think about him now it's his funeral.

I go through to the kitchen and empty out what's left of the milk. My school trousers are over the back of the chair like always, but the blazer's been hung up. I get the trousers on, then pick up the tie and pocket it. When I find the blazer I nearly pop a ball: my mother's scrubbed the armpits especially for the funeral and she's left these big white tidemarks where she didn't rinse the soap out properly. It looks like sweat-salt, for Christ's sake. I go over to the basin and soak the stuff with the dishcloth. The rings darken down okay, but when I get the blazer on I can feel the cold wet, right up there.

Outside, the light's so bright it hurts. I walk down to the bus-stop at the bottom of the street. It's so hot there's sweat prickling my head just from walking the twenty yards to the corner. I stand there, sweating and itching. I don't know when the buses are due, so I just wait and stare up the long empty road, watching all the heat waves ripple up into the air. I can smell the tarmac getting soft and behind the window I'm standing at a phone starts ringing. A red car turns the corner at the top of the street and rolls down towards me, shimmering like a mirage.

At first I think it's slowing just to turn the corner I'm stood at, so I don't take much notice until it pulls up right in front of me. I recognise the driver but she's older than me and I don't know her name or anything. Anyway, it's obvious she recognises me. She gives me this big soft smile through the open window. I smile back, but I can tell it's all wrong. I can feel it.

You know me? she says, and just then the phone inside the house stops. Her voice comes out slow and goofy, like a little kid's. It suits the weird smile which keeps coming off and on the long, white face she's got, but it doesn't suit anything else about her. The rest of her is pretty good.

Oh, hi, I say. How's it going?

She laughs, pleased for some reason and nods while she looks me up and down. I like your long hair.

Oh, I say. Jesus! I'm thinking.

You remember that horse? That horse I used to ride? She nods again, like she's encouraging me.

Maybe she's pissed or stoned, I think. But really I know it's not that. Anyway, I nod back. I saw her plenty of times riding up our street, past our window on the way to the waste-ground, Sundays and plenty of evenings after school. I've never spoken to her but so what, I think, I am now, and I'm thinking that and thinking about her on her big brown horse, jigging up and down.

The smile keeps coming and going and for what feels like a long time she just sits there, inspecting me. In the end she says: I haven't seen you around for, oh I don't know, ages. It's funny how the words sound. It's like her jaw's had some of its strings cut. Then there's the smile again, wandering onto her face like it's separate from the rest of her. Do you know what happened to me? she says suddenly. As suddenly as she can with her mouth the way it is.

No, I say. What?

She shifts her weight a little in the car seat and leans closer to me. I came off it, she says, and her smile gets fixed for a second.

Oh.

Backwards, she says.

I look up the road.

I really like your hair, she says. Are you waiting for the bus?

I turn back to her and take a good look. One of her eyes, the left one, is sort of milky looking. Apart from the milkiness, they're green. I notice her hair too. It's bunched up in little heaps over her ears and forehead, short and coppery. It's the same colour Hooper's was, which feels worrying for some reason, even in that sunlight. But she's got this nice little chin, under those wriggly lips.

It's pretty late. It might not come, I say.

She nods back, really slowly. Do you speak French? she asks.

I must look blank, because she goes straight into counting up to ten in French, like it's an explanation.

Cool, I say. It isn't what I'm thinking.

See? I can remember all my French. *Quel age est il*? That means how old are you.

I could laugh, but all of a sudden I feel like I might get somewhere if I keep playing along. Sixteen, I lie, and get a big smile of my own on.

Well, I'm twenty-one. In my body, she says carefully, lifting the finger from her lap and pointing it at her throat. But not in here, she says, and brings her finger carefully up to her temple.

I take a good look at her twenty-one year old body. She's wearing a little T-shirt and tight, faded green leggings. There are a couple of small holes in them, on the insides of her thighs, where they must rub. I can see pink shapes showing through the holes. I picture her on the horse, bouncing up and down, with her legs apart. The holes would get bigger, with all the bouncing, I think.

That old doctor, he says it might take years and years to get back to being twenty-one. She plucks around at her hair a bit. I can see down the sleeve of her T-shirt when she does it: white cotton bra with tiny blue flowers. It's nice to look at. Clean and cool. She smiles wide. Well, that's what he says, she insists, as if I'd disagreed with her. I don't know, she says. I couldn't remember a thing. That doctor. She makes a wet noise, like the start of a cough.

Everything seems fine to me. You seem fine, I lie.

Three months I was in a coma for, she says. She lifts up three fingers, then drops them dead onto the wheel. Didn't you hear about me? she asks.

She sounds surprised.

No, I say.

She nods, and I reckon it's about time I took a rest from staring at those holes, in case she notices. I start wondering if anyone realises she's out in a car, driving. I wonder if she does this most days.

I look up the road. There's a kid on a racing bike coming down the street. I know him, though he doesn't notice us and just zips past. I wonder for a second why he isn't in school. Then the white van from earlier comes down the street and pulls into the kerb a little way above my door. The same guy gets out, this time without leaflets, and starts knocking his way along the road again. Just like earlier nobody answers and soon he's worked his way to my door. I get a funny feeling watching him knock at the house, like the door's going to open, even though there's no-one home.

I couldn't remember a *thing*. Except my French, she says, shaking her head, wondering.

I look back down into the car, at her legs again, I'll admit. Then I shift closer and move a hand up to the roof of the car. It's hot as a radiator. I know it's a bad idea, with her eyes and brain the way they are, but I can't help thinking about getting my hand off that hot roof and right in there – getting some finger into those holes.

Then I think about Hooper and feel bad. In fact, I start thinking about that slab again. I even take a good look at him, on the actual slab, in my mind. But there I am, leaning against the car door, randy beyond. I go to open my mouth, but before I can speak she reaches up and takes hold of my hand and pulls it in through the window and I think Jesus, she's reading my mind, but she guides it up, not down, up to the back of her head. It feels cool after the hot roof.

Feel, she says.

The smile's flickering again now, like a lightbulb going wrong. I touch around where she's put my hand, and under all the crispy hair there's this patch of skin or bone or something, all dry and cratered, roughed up into big crusty ridges. Christ. I nearly gag it feels so bad. It's like a piece of the moon.

That doctor says, one knock there and I'm a gonner, she tells me dreamily.

I don't know what to say again so I just nod, kind of stuck there.

My horse, he had to go, she says. Then she sighs. She moves her head under my fingers, like a cat rubs against your leg.

All I can do is follow those green eyes she's got, watch them moving with her head as it nods and rolls. One clear, one milky, like something got into the water there. For some reason I leave my hand on the mess at the back of her head, but in the end she reaches behind her and takes hold, lifts it back out window. I let it hang, the nerves in my fingertips still feeling everything, and then suddenly I get a picture of the fly I saw on TV, crawling on the kid's wrist, and I'm scratching to kill the creeping in the hairs. Then I see the bus come down the street.

She doesn't move the car for the bus. I can see the driver leaning to stare down, mouthing at her, but she's miles away; light years. I walk round the front of the car to get on. I nod and hold a hand up to where she is, but the sun's dazzling on her windscreen so I can't see if she waves back, or if she even notices I've gone. I step onto the bus and it's shuddering, ready to go.

# THE SUMMERHOUSE

I

She was offered the summerhouse on her first visit to the faculty. Father
O'Brien, her graduate advisor for the four years to come, had arranged
the lease with the Dean of Divinity, Doctor Simon Hearn, who owned the
looming Gothic Revival house and riverside grounds in which the old glass
and clapboard structure stood. The white window frames and wrought-
iron porch were peeling so badly she felt pained and dimly oppressed by
her first impression of neglect; but she liked the way it nestled privately
behind a screen of Sassafras trees at the end of its own narrow, dusty dirt
path. In front of it lay nothing but open meadow and the river shining
glassy and broad some half a mile distant. The Hearns wanted just four
hundred dollars a month, and no money down.

Father O'Brien had taken it upon himself to show her the property
and clearly hoped that she would take it. They'd corresponded for months
and she realised he had taken a particular, pastoral interest in her. Look
here, he said, leading her up from the path to the summerhouse porch
and pointing out the vines twined up and over the ironwork. Small, pale
clusters of fruit bulged amongst the dark leaves and stems and on the
undersides of the leaves there were beetles clinging, their shells a startling
metallic green that shimmered as if liquid. Father O'Brien plucked one
of the grapes and rolled it between finger and thumb. Tough as a nut, he

announced. He flicked it playfully into the air and it bounced once on the path before disappearing in the long grass of the water meadow. Let's take a look inside, he suggested, and unlocked the slim French doors with an ornately old fashioned, long-stemmed key.

She knew the offer of the lease was more an act of charity than business and guessed that her circumstances must have been a topic of discussion among the staff, but she hid her embarrassment and tried to seem as professional as possible throughout the viewing. And I can keep my dog? she asked, once they'd looked the whole place over.

Oh yes, said Father O'Brien. I made sure to clear that for you. They keep dogs themselves you know, and he twitched his head in the direction of the big, vulgar house beyond the trees. Irish Wolfhounds. Fine looking beasts. He winked and smiled.

## II

On the following Sunday she moved in with Charlie, her black Labrador, again with the help of Father O'Brien. While the dog sniffed from room to room they carried in her boxes of books and bedding, panting and sweating in the afternoon sun. When Father O'Brien left to prepare for Mass at the campus chapel she inspected again each of the small, musty rooms, Charlie at her heels. The place had been vacant since the winter and when she first tried the water it ran reddish brown for almost a minute. The lavatory bowl was stained the same colour but the water itself eventually flushed clear. In the old enamel bathtub a neat line of corpses – the same small iridescent beetles she'd noticed on the vines, but dulled down by death – stretched from one end to the other like soldiers frozen in the middle of a long march. To her surprise, there were no signs of mice.

On the kitchen table was a bottle of sparkling wine and a small card propped against it.

Welcome, and God Bless your time here!
Feel free to taste our grapes but hand on heart they're NOT
good eating! Great for wine (or so they tell me!)
but the skins are tough as cow-hide!!
Just call on us if you need anything!

It was signed Jennifer B Hearn and family. A miniature dog's paw-print had been inked in underneath the word 'family'.

She put the bottle in the fridge and clamped the note to the fridge door with one of the many magnets decorating it. Most of the magnets were plain letters of the alphabet and someone had spelled out her name with them. Two flower magnets – marigolds, she thought – punctuated either end of the name and she stared at the arrangement for a while, wondering if one of the Hearn kids had come down to the summerhouse with their mother when she'd brought the note and the wine. She scrambled the letters one by one with a fingertip, then went outside to sit on the porch.

Though the big August sun was dropping low and hazy over the river the air was still laden, as it had been all day, with a disabling, sultry heat. At her back she heard the rapid tick of the dog's claws on the kitchen tiles and with a yawn he settled himself close, first sitting, then keeling onto his side and sprawling his full, glossy black length across the threshold. For a while she took hold of one of his limp front paws and ran her thumb absently over the contour lines of its hot, vinyl-like pads; then, glancing down, she saw he was wakeful, watching her with one open eye, and she let him be.

Looking more closely at the vines around her, she noticed with surprise that many of the dusty-skinned grapes were larger and riper than the one Father O'Brien had selected. She plucked a few of the largest that hung within reach then stood and clucked the dog indoors after her. After re-filling Charlie's water bowl she rinsed the grapes and set them on a shallow white dish she found in one of the cupboards.

III

That first night was too hot and unfamiliar for sleep and she lay for a long while on top of her crumpled sheets listening to her own breathing. Anticipating a stifling, restless night she had taken the grapes upstairs with her and finally she sat up, turned on the bedside lamp and chewed through them one at a time, slowly and thoughtfully.

The warning on the note was true – when she bit down the skins split a little and sloughed off the flesh without breaking up, forming leathery, tasteless packets under her teeth. Something in her revolted against swallowing them and soon she found herself working them in her mouth, furling and mashing them to pellets of slippery pulp, then teasing them open again, limp but undiminished on the tip of her tongue. In the end she picked them from between her lips and draped them over the rim of the dish.

On the wall facing the bed hung a faded print of two serious young men sitting upright but at rest in a nineteenth century scull, their oars held easy and flat over the water. They wore varsity colours and caps and she wondered if the stretch of water they were pictured on was part of the long calm flats visible from the house. A tap at the window startled her – a big river moth or beetle wanting the light. Then another, and another, like the first heavy drops before a storm. She switched the lamp off and lay back in the dark listening to occasional bird cries from the water meadows, eerie and distant. Around dawn a breeze picked up, stirring the vines into dry whispers outside the bedroom window. With the breeze seemed to come cooler air and her next memory was of being woken confusedly at noon by a sharp rapping on the glass of the French doors downstairs.

By the time she had struggled into her clothes the caller had gone, though the dog stood patiently at the door. Sorry, Charlie, she said and let him out onto the verge of the path where he squatted immediately. Following him out, she looked up the path for any sign of the caller. It was deserted, but turning back to the house she saw a smooth river rock on the porch beside the rubber doormat, and under it a letter. For a moment it confused her, then she realised the French doors had no letter slot and there was no mailbox on the path outside.

The letter was from her father and she sat herself on the porch to read it. He was worried about her and wanted to speak to her. Would she phone or find time to visit again soon or even just write? Why had she left early on the weekend? She had been welcome to stay until the semester began. Surely she knew that? Anyway, that was what he'd expected her to do. There were still important things he wanted to know. There were things he wanted to ask her.

She folded it before reaching the end and called the dog back indoors. She poured herself a bowl of cereal.

The visit to her father's the weekend before had exhausted her and she had no intention of repeating it. Marian, his second wife, was just a few years older than herself and had only been with him for six years but already they had three raucous kids and another on the way. She'd been one of his last patients before he gave up his practice. Now, like some throwback pioneer he spent most of his free time building timber forts, jungle gyms, tree-houses, even an open-air bathhouse in their sprawling back garden, though the kids were too young for any of it. Marian just seemed to wander dazedly from kitchen to outdoor Jacuzzi and back again in various states of undress. The kids ran wild at all hours of the day, she hadn't been allowed to take Charlie, and the bathrooms had no locks.

On the afternoon she'd left, Marian had wanted her to try the outdoor bathhouse. Just peel right off and get on in, she'd said. This sun's so hot and the garden's private, there's no one can see.

Don't you get drowned bugs washing around in there? she'd wanted to know, and Marian laughed.

It took some time and a growing unpleasantness in the atmosphere between them but finally Marian gave up with a shrug and stripped completely there and then on the lawn. She picked her way barefoot over to the sunken tub, trailed by Nathan, the middle kid, a demanding boy of three. She bent from the waist and twisted some kind of lever to set the water churning.

Don't know what you're missing, missy, she called, and lowered her short, plump nakedness until only her grinning head was visible.

The boy Nathan left his mother and came running to where she sat on the lawn. He took hold of her right hand as if to pull her upright and she smiled and stood for him. Where do you want to go? she said, but he dropped her hand and instead took hold of her light print skirt. What is it? she said, but he had no interest in her now other than to tug at the skirt. She stared down at his scowling, determined face, feeling the elastic waistband slip to the broadest span of her hips, dragging her underpants with it. Stooping, she prised away the soft, sticky buds of his fists and strode quickly back to the house.

In the cool privacy of her room she readjusted herself and then moved to the window. In the garden Marian was out of the tub, still naked, chasing both Nathan and the oldest child, an intelligent, wilful little madam of five, around the bathhouse. All three of them were shrieking.

Beyond them, in the shadow of his timber fort, her father was sawing lengths of plank for some new project. His long, curly grey hair and the grey wooliness of his torso were ringletted with sweat. His chest was like the underside of an animal, of a sheep or a goat, she had often thought when a child. Below it his paunch bulged over the waistband of his jeans shorts, a sudden, comical swelling, abrupt as a blister above his skinny loins.

She had packed hurriedly, called a cab and left a note on the kitchen table with her apologies and thanks.

## IV

After a salad lunch she took the dog for a long walk beside the river. When she returned, Father O'Brien was waiting on the porch, his long legs stretched out and crossed comfortably at the ankles. He waved as they approached, his eyes hidden behind sunglasses.

Inside, he asked how she was settling in and made a fuss of Charlie.

She took the cold bottle of wine from the fridge and set it on the kitchen table. While she searched for two glasses he said, I can open it with this, and with a comic flourish unfolded a corkscrew from his penknife. She set out the glasses and sat opposite him and he poured the wine. They drank and spoke of the hot weather for a while.

You know, he said, reaching down to the dog at his feet and dragging his nails against the grain of the fur along its stomach, I once had a Labrador much like Charlie.

Oh, she said, pleased.

Not everyone appreciated him, though. I was a full time parochial priest in those days and one of my flock, a very troubled young man, came to me for advice of an evening. Without a thought, you understand, I sat him on the couch with the dog at his feet. Well now, he said, and took another long swallow of wine, warming to his story. Well now, this boy, he patted and stroked that dog as if his very soul depended on it. He nearly smoothed that dog to a pattern in the carpet, by God. O'Brien paused and smiled a little shyly at her.

She smiled back.

Well now, it was only some time later when this boy rose up to go and I shook his hand that I realised his palm was completely fouled with sweat and black fur. Feugh! It was matted, literally *matted* with that poor dog's hair.

He paused again for effect and she widened her eyes.

That boy had been so fearful of dogs he'd been close on crushing it to protect himself! O'Brien shook his head and drained his glass before refilling it. I know the fear of God is the beginning of wisdom, he said, but I don't know what the fear of dogs might signify. He let out a short laugh. Now how about that, he concluded, and gave a couple of hearty slaps to Charlie's broad, upturned ribcage.

She could find nothing to say but held her smile until he'd finished shaking his head and grinning at the memory. There was silence for a while and she wondered if she should rise and switch on the light.

I enjoyed reading your research proposal, he said at last. I think it's full of promise.

Thank you, she said.

He nodded drowsily. You've read Coleridge? The philosophy, I mean.

She shook her head.

Ah, he said.

## V

On the Wednesday she took a bus into town. Outside the drug store an alarmingly thin, middle-aged man with a gentle but distracted manner was handing out flyers to anyone who would take them. He wore sandals, baggy linen shorts and a spotless sky-blue T-shirt. On the bus ride back to the campus she read through the leaflet.

> My name is **PAUL**. In 1971 after a bad experience with hallucinogenic drugs I developed mental difficulties. My medication **BURNS** the nerve-endings in my brain and prevents the **NATURAL HEALING** process taking place. If you can offer me **SAFE HAVEN** where I can stop my medication and allow **NATURAL HEALING** to take place please contact me on: 888-1359

She read over it again in the kitchen of the summerhouse, then with a strawberry magnet fixed it to the fridge door.

As evening came on she gave up on her books and sat outside with Charlie. She picked a handful of grapes but they seemed more bitter than before and after chewing the juice from them she spat the skins out onto the dirt path. Out on the water meadows she could see one of the Hearn kids, a young girl, walking two of the wolfhounds. In the distance, against the low sun, the great, loping dogs seemed weirdly gaunt and stylized, like cave paintings brought to a brief, twilight life. No sound carried from them and even Charlie seemed unaware of their passing.

When it grew too dark to see the river she stood and stepped down to the path. Charlie, she said, and tossed him one of the grapes. He snapped at it and, to her surprise, not only gulped it down but lifted his head expectantly, eager for more. Amused, she lobbed another towards his muzzle, knowing that the next day she would study his stools for the skins.

### VI

The next morning she woke at first light from a nightmare of vomiting up, wrenchingly, a long, burning stream of undigested grape skins. When she lifted her face away from the hot dent of her pillow she was astonished to see dry, unsoiled sheets surrounding her. Her stomach throbbed from the violence of retching and the stink of bile seemed real in her nostrils but when she touched her lips they were clean. She caught sight of the white dish still sitting by the side of the bed. The skins clinging to its rim were desiccated now: hard, waxy and smooth like fingernails.

Dazed, she let her head fall back to the pillow and suddenly remembered helping her mother bring in washing from the clothesline in the big, windy backyard of her childhood home. The bed sheets needed folding and as they each took their corners a rain of tiny black beetles fell from the opened folds. They seemed to wake on landing and swarmed for new shelter in the cracked paving around her feet. Her mother, always so nervous, had jumped back, shrieking, and dropped her end of the sheet. Later that day, eyes wide with drama and disgust, her mother had kept saying to her over and over again: But what if we hadn't noticed? My God, what if we'd put that sheet back on the bed with all those black bugs on it?

And lying on her own bed now she heard the dog scratching and keening at the door and felt the skin of her bare legs crawl with tiny pincers and limbs. She clenched her thighs, her whole body rigid under the covers. She'd been nine or ten, but even at that age had known with an awful, childish sense of doom that it was a crazy thing for an adult to be saying, a crazy way to think.

How could you *not* notice? she'd demanded at last, and already her young throat had felt as if it might choke on fury and despair.

# THERE IS A SAVIOUR

Leyden had seen her naked once, slipping out of his son's room in the small dark hours of a winter's morning, padding cat-like to the bathroom door. It was towards the end of the school term and he'd been working through the night, bleary-eyed and wired on caffeine at the kitchen table, marking exam scripts. She'd glanced up the long hall towards the light but hadn't noticed or hadn't cared about him staring back at her over his stacks of papers. Embarrassed, he'd got up and moved out of sight of the hallway, then waited a while after the flush had been pulled to be sure she'd had time to flit back.

That had been early in her stay, just a week or so after she'd moved in to share a room, and bed, with his nineteen-year-old student son, Matthew. After a long, bitter quarrel with the boy that had made him feel morally petty for objecting to the girl's arrival, he'd finally given in, realising, even as they raged at one another, that a part of him was intrigued by the idea – was hungry for any change in their deadlocked, fierce life together. After saving face with a few petty rules and restrictions he'd allowed the two youngsters to get on with their arrangement, secretly fascinated.

To his surprise, he'd soon found himself actually enjoying the extra presence in the roomy, unhomely Edinburgh flat. Though he rarely saw the girl, Emma, other than in passing, and even then never exchanged more than a few polite words with her, he sensed a contentment about her, a stability that seemed to make the flat a busier but much more placid space than it had been before. The ugly silences he'd often endured with just Matthew for company became almost a thing of the past, though the boy still communicated only when necessary, and never with warmth. Above all, Leyden enjoyed having the tokens of a woman's presence around him after years of living without them: the bewildering toiletries in the bathroom, pastel buntings of underwear on the radiators, the scent of lotions or perfume sometimes lingering in the hallway.

Then, after six peaceful months, without warning Matthew decided that Emma had to leave. Typically, the boy had explained nothing but asked Leyden, in a tersely written note pinned to his bedroom door, to drive her home to Kettick, a small fishing town on the east coast. It would be a four hundred mile round trip at least, Leyden knew, maybe half of it on slow country roads; but his son had never learned how to drive and over the winter months the girl had moved in much more than she could manage on a train or bus. Gripped by a fury he couldn't fully explain to himself, Leyden had stalked through the flat, hoping to find the boy alone. But the couple were out or lying low behind their locked bedroom door and for the girl's sake he resigned himself to a long, embarrassing journey.

That Saturday morning, Leyden collected the hired van he'd booked and drove it back through a cold, light drizzle to the pile of luggage, boxes and plastic bags Matthew had brought down from the flat. The youngsters were standing watch over the boxes, careless of the rain. They stood hand in hand, Leyden noted, and a surge of distaste towards his son made him turn his face away as they approached the van. There was a bang against the side of the vehicle – the flat of a palm – and he heard Matthew shout for him to come and unlock the doors.

Neither of the youngsters seemed willing to make eye contact with Leyden as he joined them on the pavement and hauled back the van's big, sliding side-door. You should get in the cab out of the wet, he said to Emma. We'll see to the loading.

Ignoring him, she detached herself from Matthew and took hold of one of the suitcases. A freshening breeze was tugging at the plastic bags amongst the boxes, rustling them and flinging cold drops of heavier rain.

Okay, Leyden said, as if to himself, and set to work alongside her. For a few moments the boy watched them, blankly, then followed their lead.

Once the loading was done, Leyden climbed inside and waited at the wheel while they got through their goodbyes. The rain, strengthening all the time, had begun to drum onto the roof of the cab and when she heaved herself up into the passenger seat Emma's long dark hair was lank and dripping. She gasped as she sat back, wiping the wetness from her forehead. There was a whiff of spirits on her breath and Leyden looked across at her, searching her face for signs of what to expect in the hours to come. Her smooth, pale, distracted face gave nothing away. As Leyden indicated to pull out from the kerb she squirmed to stare out at Matthew. Hunched and grimacing under the downpour he offered up a perfunctory wave, and Leyden again felt an upswell of exasperation and shame.

Thanks for the lift, she said, turning from the window once they were out of sight of the tenement.

He shrugged and cleared his throat. Listen, he said, I'm sorry about all this – the way he's acted. He wet his lips. Getting you home safe and sound is the least I can do. The collars of his shirt and jacket were wet through after the loading and as he moved his head to address her he felt the cotton rub against his throat. She wasn't looking at him, she was looking straight ahead. He turned his own eyes back to the road and shivered. The rain was washing down hard onto the windscreen and the inside of the glass was clouded with moisture from their wet skin and clothes. It was hard to see out into the traffic. He turned the fan heater to high and the cab filled with the sound of rushing air.

Shifting in her seat she stared hard at him for a while. There's no need to be sorry, she said, raising her voice to be heard over the fan. Matty just needs some time; then we'll get married properly and be back together again for good.

Surprised by the authority in her voice, Leyden glanced across at her. You think so?

She nodded once, decisively.

Well, that's good. If you think you're ready for all that.

She made no reply and in the awkward lull Leyden was suddenly aware not just of the heater's loud blast of air but also, behind it, the churning electric motor driving the windscreen wipers. He listened to it flailing the blades against each swill of rain. He knew without looking at her that he had made some mistake.

You don't believe me, do you? she said abruptly. You think I'm just being young and naïve.

153

No, he said. I didn't say that. He turned the fan down to a lower setting. He could feel his temperature beginning to rise and with a finger loosened the damp collar of his shirt where it stuck to his neck. She was still facing him, he realised, though he didn't turn to make eye-contact. He caught another trace of alcohol on the stuffy air and wondered grimly how much she had drunk.

Matty told me you don't believe in anything, she said, as if noting the weather. He said you're too bitter. He told me you're the most cynical person I'll ever meet.

For a long, stunned moment, Leyden replayed the girl's words in his head. He heard himself laugh, humourlessly. Heat was spreading over him now, prickling at his scalp and neck. Did he? he managed to say. He nodded as if in approval. And what does Matthew believe in then?

She was doing something with her hair. Out of the corner of his eye he caught glimpses of her bare white forearm rising and sweeping back. She took her time answering, then said simply, Matty's very spiritual.

Spiritual! he almost blurted, but checked himself. He nodded again instead, labouring for some response that might put a quick stop to the conversation.

That's why we've got to be apart for a while, she went on.

Leyden realised he was still nodding, and stopped himself. Matthew was always the… serious type, he managed at last.

At noon he turned off into a service station and asked her if she was hungry, taking a close look at her face again. She had pulled her hair back tight over her scalp, knotting and pinning it above the nape of her neck. She looked very white and distant and shook her head when Leyden repeated the question.

Well I'm getting a coffee at least, maybe something to eat, he told her.

I'll go to the Ladies, she said, opening her door.

Okay. I'll be in the Burger King. He followed her through the rain across the car park and into the foyer.

He was already eating at one of the window tables by the time she came to find him. She eased herself into the cramped seating opposite him and smiled. She looked better, Leyden thought, now that there was colour in her cheeks.

I was sick, she announced. I had a drink this morning before we left.

She laid a hand over her stomach. I feel fine now, though. I'll get a burger too.

I'll get it, he mumbled through a full mouth, but she was already freeing herself from the table.

Across from him a burly, shaven-headed man was struggling into his seat. His thickly muscled arms and neck were blue with crudely drawn tattoos – a death's-head, slogans in gothic script, swastikas. The man ate slowly, thoughtfully, staring straight ahead.

Emma returned with two small plain burgers and a milk shake. She bolted them quickly but neatly, dispatching one after the other with just a few swift, precise bites. Once the food was gone she slowed down, dawdling over the drink. Twice Leyden caught her eyeing him as he turned from staring out at the rain. She smiled briefly each time and then looked down at her drink, or across at the skinhead's tattooed arms and neck.

Still feeling okay? Leyden asked finally.

Much better. I just needed to be sick. She laughed self-deprecatingly.

He smiled, glad that the silence was broken.

For a while she stared at the skinhead again, then turned back to Leyden. How long were you married? she asked.

Leyden frowned but managed to keep smiling. He reflected for a while, looking sidelong at her open, strangely impassive face, realising with some surprise that he felt a growing sense of pleasure at the thought of being open, perhaps a little vulnerable, with this peculiar, awkwardly mannered girl. Maybe somewhere inside her, underneath all the callowness, lay a seed of sympathy, even recognition. The thought pleased him, but in a way that made him shift nervously in his plastic seat. Fifteen years, he said.

That's a long time.

He shrugged, faintly gratified by her response. It sounds a long time when you're young.

Her mouth twisted into a thin half-smile and once again he knew he had slipped. Sensing what was coming next, he braced himself.

Why did it go wrong? She took a draw on her milkshake, her eyes fixing him. Do you mind me asking?

No, he laughed. No, I don't mind. It's, ah, water under the bridge. He paused as if to reflect though he knew exactly what he was about to say. He cleared his throat. We just married too young, etcetera etcetera, you know. The old story. To his surprise he realised he was blushing and his chest had grown tight.

She was nodding but her gaze was penetrating now, maybe puzzled, Leyden thought, or maybe critical. He shifted again in his tiny seat, wishing he'd never let the conversation happen.

But if you'd been right for one another, then marrying young wouldn't have mattered. She placed her milkshake on the table between them like a checkmate.

Leyden regarded her. Well. She was kind to me at a bad time in my life, he said. That can mean a lot to you when you're young. Too much, probably. He shrugged. Anyway, people make mistakes. And people *change*, he said, glad to have thought suddenly of that final, conclusive truth.

She screwed her face into a quick sceptical grimace, then relaxed it. After a long pause she said, I think it's good that Matty and me have broken up for a while now. We'll be stronger because of it when we get back together. With her fingertips she shifted the tall paper beaker of milk across the table in small zigzags. Matty thinks so too. He said he never wants to do to me what you did to his mother.

Leyden winced. So that's it, he thought. That's what it's all about. Back to the boy. Of course – it should have been obvious to him. Well, I don't know, he said. But we ought to get moving.

Outside, the rain had eased and as he walked between the rows of parked cars to the van Leyden felt grateful for the fine, needling coolness it brought to his face. Ahead of him he recognised the shaved head of the tattooed man. He was covered by his jacket now and was getting into a white van like theirs. A sudden cold slap of wind made Leyden shiver and he jogged the last yards, hearing her footsteps keep pace on the wet tarmac behind.

In the cab of the van he sat still for a few moments, gathering his thoughts while she rearranged her hair again, this time freeing it from its knot but then tying it back into a long, slack pony-tail. She half turned her head, eyeing him. I had alopecia when I was little. All my hair fell out. She was slicking her hands over her scalp now, over the tight wet strands.

Oh, he said.

It used to come away in clumps. I'd be playing with my hair and stop to look and my hands would be full of all this long black hair. You never feel it coming out. She smiled oddly at him. I screamed the first time it happened.

For a moment he met her gaze then turned back to face the windscreen, feeling suddenly too tired for words. But he had to speak, he supposed. What was the cure? he said at last.

She shrugged, still smoothing around her skull. It was just nerves – it went away in the end. She yawned. Did you see the man at the table next to us? With the tattoos?

Leyden nodded, finding himself yawning also, triggered by the girl. *Shut up*, he needed to tell her, but of course he couldn't. *Shut up now, please, and for Christ's sake just let me drive.* He sighed.

It's really weird. Matty told me a story just last week about someone exactly like that – a skinhead, really violent and racist and everything. His minister told him about it.

His minister?

At his church.

Leyden closed his eyes. Oh, Christ. What church? What minister? He listened to her voice tumbling on, light and life in her face for the first time that day, and wished he could get out into the cool rain; maybe lie under it; let it wash down and drown out all this embarrassing nonsense. Through a kind of daze he followed her story about a tattooed young skinhead cut out of a car wreck by a black fireman. The fireman saw his Nazi tattoos and witnessed to him about Jesus, she was saying, while he was cutting him out. He had to keep him talking to keep him alive, this black fireman. He was the only survivor – she'd forgotten to say that, at the start. And he was a minister now, in London, she was telling him, using his tattoos as a witness. He could have had them removed but he used them as a witness, now.

Leyden grunted. There was silence for a while. Finally he slotted the key into the ignition.

You don't believe in any of that, do you? she said.

He felt himself frown.

I'm not saved either. But at least I've got an open mind. How can you explain what happens to people like that otherwise? If there isn't a saviour?

Leyden opened his mouth but said nothing. Why was she provoking him like this? Every time she opened her mouth, another trial, another challenge. Some kind of displacement, maybe. Anger at Matthew. Yes. It had to be that.

But you don't know, do you? Just because *you* don't believe doesn't mean there isn't anything to believe. Maybe there is a saviour.

Maybe, then, he said at last, losing all patience. I don't know. But even if there *is*, he spat, his voice rising helplessly, what the hell would *he* know? What the hell would *Matthew* know about it? He twisted to stare her down.

She shrank back into her corner but forced an angry smile. That's a terrible thing to say, she said quietly. And don't shout at me.

He breathed a miserable, embarrassed laugh and a gust of wind swept the car park, quivering the van. He waited a minute or so, letting his head clear. Sorry, he said, and started the engine. Turning to her, he saw she was close to tears.

Matty said you were a bully. And a coward. Her voice was strangled but she swallowed hard and carried on. I always thought that was a mean thing to say. But now I think he was right.

Leyden frowned. I don't care what he thinks, he said firmly. I don't even know what he means. Listen, he said, he's thrown all kinds of shit at me over the years and it doesn't stick any more. He paused for a while, staring out at the car park. The skinhead in his white van was still there a few rows ahead of them. He hadn't even started his engine. What was he waiting for? Leyden turned to face her. And it doesn't matter to me what *you* think, he finished.

Her eyes narrowed a fraction and a flicker of gratification passed through Leyden like a current. Well it's obvious what *you* think. It's obvious you think I'm stupid because I'm too young to know any better. But maybe you're the stupid one because you're too old.

Too old for what? Despite himself he began to laugh.

To listen to anybody else! It was her turn to play fierce now, he realised, and his laugh set into a grim smile.

I don't know. Whatever, he said. Then, studying her again, and curious suddenly, how old *are* you, anyway? he asked.

She took an old, wadded tissue from her jeans pocket and blew her nose wetly. Sixteen, she said through cupped hands.

What?

Nearly seventeen.

Leyden blinked as if shaking off sleep, a sharp thrill of alarm twisting his stomach. Christ! he said.

So? she challenged, but without confidence.

I didn't know that. He breathed in and out once, slowly. If I'd known that I'd never have let you move in with him. Sixteen! Christ! he said again.

She snorted but shifted uncomfortably in her seat.

How can you be at university? I thought you met Matthew there?

I never said I was. I said I was a student. I'm doing my Highers at Telford.

Highers! He shook his head, a tight, angry grin locking the muscles of his face.

It doesn't matter.

It matters to me!

It's none of your business.

None of my business? He shook his head, a strange, excited outrage uncoiling inside him. You lived under my roof like a married woman, all these months, he said, hearing his voice rise in pitch again, and you're just a kid… just a wee *schoolgirl* for Christ's sakes.

I'm not a child! And you can let me out if all you can do is shout at me again. She braced herself against the door, but made no attempt to open it.

He took a deep breath, trembling, shocked at his own arousal. Now that the first hot flare of prurience was dying away he had a sudden sensation of absolute clarity. Everything she'd said that day, every absurd statement, every gesture and inflection seemed to replay in an instant behind his eyes. Just a kid. Of course. All the bizarre mystical arrogance – just precociousness. Just childishness after all. A kind of helplessness really, he thought, and felt a sharp pang of superiority and pity towards the frail, cornered creature at his side. An acute consciousness of his male, adult bulk swelled within him, a sense of his heavy flesh and bone, full grown; all its stolid, controlling power. Well, he said, and looked her in the eye. Do your parents know? What do they think about it? He opened his mouth to question her again but stopped himself, not trusting his voice to conceal his triumphalism now.

There's only my father, she said flatly.

Oh, he said, and paused. So what does he think?

She leaned her head against the window and didn't answer.

I know what I'd think, he breathed, and shook his head.

By the time they rejoined the motorway she was sobbing freely and as he listened to each long, shuddering release it occurred to Leyden that in the wake of his new mastery over her, what he felt wasn't anger or disapproval, nor just simple pity for the way he'd made her feel now, but something more like foreboding; like dread. What were these passions she'd stirred up in him? How had she known how to do it? And *why* do it, anyway? He understood women very poorly, he knew. How long had it been since he'd even spoken to a woman in anything other than a professional or indifferent way? Apart from a few half-hearted flirtations at work, and one awful, drunken humiliation – more years than he cared to number. Five or six, maybe. Nowadays, he rarely bothered making the effort to go out for anything other than his chess club and occasional concerts. Jesus, what was wrong with him? But was he lonely? Was he frustrated? No. Never. And what the hell was wrong with self-sufficiency, anyway? What was wrong with some quiet, adult dignity, in circumstances like his? What had caused this whole scene now, if it wasn't his own damned son's overheated, adolescent fever for every kind of intimacy?

An overwhelming impulse to remonstrate with the girl, to justify his chosen life – *chosen*, dammit! – was building like a blockage in his throat. He fought it back, unclenching his jaw, knowing the need was misplaced. She wouldn't have any idea what he was talking about. The very thought was grotesque; chaotic. But it was there: the urge.

And what had she meant by calling him a bully and a coward? What had Matthew meant by it? Years of learning to harden his heart against all that kind of blame and bitterness from the boy; why was it cutting into him now? Why a coward? A bully? He'd never hit the boy. Not once. Even through all the worst times when by Christ he would have been justified. More than justified! Who had he ever bullied in fact? One child, maybe. A cheeky, backward young boy he had lost all patience with in his probationary year of teaching. Just as the marriage was starting to fall apart, of course. No coincidence there, and he was green then, too, in his dealings with kids. Years of bank work had done nothing to prepare him for a classroom rustling with sniggers and whispers. He hadn't struck the brat, but kept him back and hurt him, yes, one day after class. Took hold of his collar hard and shook him off his feet like a pup, or a rat. Sheer luck it never came to light. But Matthew, no. Matthew he'd never hurt – Matthew who'd so often deserved it.

With an effort he woke himself from his trance. He was speeding and could remember nothing of the last few miles of road. Slowing the van he tried to relax his bunched, aching shoulders. It was sadness, not violence inside him, he thought, not danger. Dull, lumpen misery, and guilt for things he hadn't meant and things he couldn't change, like a great tumour on his heart. And who except Matthew would damn him for that? He opened his window and for a while let the cold sodden air rush into the cabin. Greedily he breathed it in, smelling the soaked earth, the open, indifferent land outside, letting his self-pity subside. Then he remembered her thin, bare arms and closed the glass again.

Sorry, he said, but there was no answer.

An early, raw twilight was closing in on the narrow roads as they made the last stretch of the journey along the coast. After crying bitterly but briefly Emma had turned the radio on then slept for a long while, or at least pretended to. On waking she seemed calm again, even friendly, much to Leyden's surprise. She seemed content to chat to him, all provocation gone from her voice, pointing out the ways to ancient standing stones, the road to a fishing village abandoned since the war. Leyden made an effort to seem attentive, grateful for the changed atmosphere, but it was difficult to concentrate on her words or even his own thoughts. Now that she was speaking again the overwhelming gloom he'd felt earlier had returned, had found him out and taken hold of him like a tide around a tired swimmer, though he couldn't say why. Each time the great, grey shifting slabs of the North Sea hove into view he felt his heart lurch and chill as if his road ended out there amongst them.

Just inside Kettick he paused at traffic lights. At the crossing a small girl, oblivious to the rain, was swinging an empty plastic carrier bag out in front of her to catch and be pulled by the gusting wind. He could hear her shrieks each time she was yanked forwards. Other than the child the street ahead seemed empty.

You need to take the next left, Emma said. She was watching the girl too, but without expression. We're nearly there now, she added.

Soon they entered an ugly, unkempt cul-de-sac where the sandstone Victorian buildings of the High Street gave way to a cluster of modern, concrete-clad flats. There, she said, and pointed to one of the doorways. You can park right up close. My dad's too old to help with the unloading, she warned.

That's fine, Leyden muttered. He bumped the van up onto the pavement near the entrance then killed the engine.

She smoothed a hand over her hair. I'll go up and tell him we're here. Then I'll come and help.

Okay.

She hesitated a moment. He'll want you to stay for a while, to meet you.

Leyden stared at her, dismayed. I'd rather head back. Once everything's in.

He'll think you're rude if you don't. She opened her door and swung out before he could answer.

The radio was playing but had lost its signal somewhere along the coast. He hadn't noticed while they were talking, what with the noise of the engine and the rain. Now, alone and with the engine dead he listened to it crackling softly, unearthly in the gloom. He switched it off and lowered himself stiff-limbed from the cabin. He unlocked and dragged back with a long, low rumble the heavy side-door of the van. For a moment he paused, leaning against the cold wet panel, then started hauling her belongings out onto a narrow, sheltered porch. Finally Emma appeared, propping the door open with a box before stepping out to help.

He was sleeping, she said. He does want to meet you, though. You're to come up for some tea before you drive back.

Leyden puffed his cheeks. I don't know. It's getting late.

I've already wet the tea, she said. She crouched to lift a couple of boxes then started for the concrete stairs.

He grunted as he took the weight of a pair of suitcases, then followed her in.

The flat was on the second floor. The hall was badly lit and smelled strongly of pipe smoke. The aroma was pleasant but somehow saddening and a sudden qualm of regret and loss swept through Leyden. Almost overwhelmed, he paused for a moment, as if to catch his breath, waiting for the strange, powerful feeling to pass. There was no sign of the father. She signalled to him to take the luggage into an empty bedroom to his left. He carried the cases in, wondering if the room had been hers before she'd left home. There were no pictures on the plain-papered walls or books on the shelves and the mattress on the narrow bed was covered by just a taut white cotton sheet. He slid the cases against a wall and was glad to get back out of the flat and into the cold bright space of the concrete stairwell.

By the time they'd finished Leyden was clammy with sweat and impatient to be gone, though with a sense of guilty responsibility he allowed the girl to lead him along the hall into a narrow, low-ceilinged living room. Like the hall, the atmosphere was loaded with pungent, sweetish pipe smoke, obscurely familiar.

An old man began pushing himself out of his deep armchair as they entered the room. Here you are then, he said. Though heavily built, and obviously old enough to be the girl's grandfather, he moved easily to where the two of them stood. He held out a broad, doughy hand for Leyden to shake. Sit yourself down, he wheezed. He rattled out a quick, loose cough, his jowls quivering.

Leyden moved in the big man's wake to a low couch. Sinking into it he felt its broken softness draw him down and back. The father peered at him with a mild, sleepily satisfied expression, then followed Emma through a door into what seemed to be the kitchen. A big, boxy old TV in the corner was showing a football match, the volume turned down to a murmur. Directly in front of him an old-fashioned gas fire was burning fitfully, sputtering and hissing almost as loudly as the ghostly cheering and chanting from the game. The waves of heat from it were pleasant on his feet and legs. He yawned and sank back deeper into the spongy cushions, allowing his eyes to close. Jesus, he thought, I could black out forever. With an effort he opened his eyes and forced himself to concentrate on the football. Soon the father was back again, handing Leyden a mug of strong sweet tea. Well now, he said thickly, and lowered himself, grunting, onto the couch. There was no sign of the girl.

To begin with Leyden felt revived by the hot tea, but after the first few mouthfuls its heat and sweetness seemed to bloom inside him with the same narcotic force as the fire. He listened as if through a thick curtain of sleep, as the low, moist, unhurried voice of the girl's father asked him simple questions about the drive up, the weather, life in the city. With difficulty, Leyden answered him, hardly conscious of some of his replies. He was aware of the scrape of a match and the sharp brief stink of its sulphur, then the cloying fragrance of the old man's tobacco rolled across him like incense. Again he felt the pang of some hidden, childhood loss.

Some long dead, forgotten figure, at the farthest edge of memory – not his father, surely, who had never smoked, or taken pleasure in any such thing, as far as Leyden could remember – but who, then?

See this, now, the old man said quietly, nodding towards the TV.

With an effort, Leyden lifted his slumped head and watched as the old man cycled through channels with a remote control. Satellite, ken? he confided. He stopped at a channel and gestured for Leyden to pay attention to it. It was pornography, but just a series of teasers for films showing later that night. The clips were so brief and close-up that Leyden found himself struggling to make sense of the glimpsed flesh and hard, concentrated faces.

Satellite, he heard the father intone again, soft and sly. Special viewing card. Fae Europe, so it's double-dutch, ken? The old man chuckled, coughed wetly, then raced back through the channels to the football.

Letting his head drop back down, Leyden closed his eyes. He had to leave soon, he knew. If he let himself get any drowsier he'd have to find somewhere to spend the night. With each mouthful of tea prickles of sweat were rising across his forehead. Hazily, he wondered if he was not just tired but sick; fevered, maybe.

So then, ye've kent ma quine a whiley now? The question was friendly but there was something measured, a hint of cunning in the tone that made Leyden straighten himself and concentrate on his answer.

Six months, he agreed. Since November. He cleared his throat a little nervously. Was this the beginning of the rebuke, father to father? he wondered. He had already decided not to defend himself, or his son. He would listen passively, accept every judgement. Maybe he would stay completely silent through it all, rise calmly at the end and go. He didn't know. It was complicated somehow by her father being so much older than he'd expected. Battling against the warm fog in his mind he opened his mouth to speak, then halted, saying nothing.

Another match flared up to his right as the old man re-lit his pipe. And fit is it ye dae then?

I teach, he said.

Oho, a teacher, he said, and half chuckled, half coughed, rattling a thick chain of phlegm deep in his chest. So is that how ye met then, aye?

Leyden stared at the fire, his understanding slowed by its lapping heat and the billows of thick sweet tobacco smoke. He shook his head at last.

No, no. It's not like that, he mumbled. We're not...

The father held up his broad, white hand and shook his head benevolently.

In Leyden's mind an image of his son formed, but it was featureless, like an effigy worn smooth. He had to speak about the boy, of course. But why did his own son's name catch in his throat now? And where was the girl for Christ's sake, to set the old man right? He felt his eyelids closing and forced them back open. Dimly, he was aware of the father saying something about tiredness, about staying the night. Leyden shook his head, but the old man was already up from the couch, was moving away towards the kitchen.

What was happening to him? He was caught here, absurdly, like some accidental prodigal. With a new sense of urgency he struggled from the clasp of the soft cushions to stand upright, queasy and unsteady. Behind a pair of heavy drape curtains near the TV he found a tall sash window and battled to open it, finally forcing it up a few inches. Outside, the rain was falling straight, washing onto the van below, onto the street and onto the grey blocks of flats all around like the beginning of an endless, final flood. It was impossible to imagine the road home – when he tried, all he saw in his mind's eye was the rain, falling in swathes as if the journey lay not over roads and mapped land but a wilderness of water.

Sensing movement at his back, Leyden turned to find the father at his elbow. He was staring impassively past him, out into the rainswept dark. The old man nodded. There now, mannie, see that, he said, his voice a low, complacent drone. There's nae call to journey in that.

The kitchen door opened and Emma stepped through, pausing there to watch the two men. She had changed into a plain white cotton shift that fell almost to her bare feet and her hair was bound up in a white towel. Like a kelpie, eh? Leyden heard the old man mumble admiringly. Like a kelpie fae the sea. She smiled distractedly and turned back into the kitchen again. As if obeying some hidden signal, the old man left Leyden and followed her out of sight. An image of the empty bedroom he'd carried her luggage into flashed through Leyden's mind and he shivered as if chilled. He saw the bare narrow bed again; the empty walls. He moved back to the couch and sat forward on it, hungry for the heat of the fire. Finally he sank back and allowed sleep to overtake him.

He woke suddenly, heart racing, from a dream of speaking with the ghost of his wife. He knew it had grown late. A solid darkness filled the gap in the drape curtains where earlier he'd stood. Aware of a presence behind him he arched his neck and saw the girl's face looking down at him. She smiled faintly as their eyes met and he slumped back into the cushions.

You were whimpering, she said, and he understood that she had woken him.

Leyden bowed his head. In the wake of his dream he felt a sense of renunciation and calm, though he had no clear understanding of what it was he might have renounced. The gas fire was still hissing at his feet. He tried to speak, but his dry tongue felt heavy and dead as sun-warmed wood or stone. Looking up again, he saw the silent bulk of the girl's father framed by the light in the kitchen doorway. Was he watching them? His expression was empty as a carved Buddha's. The eyes were open but it seemed the face of a sleeping man, face of all sleeping fathers. Leyden closed his own eyes, wearily, and knew he would not be leaving.

## Acknowledgements

I am grateful for the suggestions of several careful readers of some or all of these stories, including Ali Lumsden, Brian McCabe, Alan Spence, Adrian Searle and Alan Warner. I would also like to thank the editors of the following publications where the stories first appeared, sometimes in different versions: *The Aberdeen Review, Causeway/Cabhsair, Carve Magazine, Edinburgh Review, The Fish Anthology* (2007), *Gutter, New Writing Scotland* (10 & 18), Route Publishing's *Book at Bedtime* and *Bonne Route* anthologies, and *Shorts: The Macallan/Scotland on Sunday Short Story Collection* (1999 & 2000).

'Everywhere Was Water Once' was a prize-winner in the Fish International Short Story Competition in 2007; 'Underworld' was shortlisted in the Bridport International Short Story Competition in 2007; 'Rain' and 'There Is a Saviour' were shortlisted for the Raymond Carver Short Story Prize in 2006; 'A Piece of the Moon' and 'Dead of Winter' were runners-up in The Macallan/Scotland on Sunday Short Story Competitions of 1999 and 2000 respectively.

My grateful thanks are also due to the Scottish Book Trust for providing me with a New Writer Award in 2010/11.